Cat Killed A Rat

Ponderosa Pines Cozy Mystery Series
Book 1

Erin Lynn
ReGina Welling

Cat Killed A Rat

ISBN- 978-1517516307
ISBN- 1517516307

Cover art by: L. Vryhof
Interior design by: L. Vryhof

www.reginawelling.com
http://erinlynnwrites.com

First Edition
Printed in the U.S.A.

Erin Lynn

From the author:

First and foremost, I want to thank my amazing co-author and mother for bearing with me through this process. It's been an incredible experience, and I absolutely could not have done it without you!

To my precious boys, Kash & Wyatt: this is, as are all the things I do, for you.

Thank you Alexander, for also bearing with me, and being there for me always.

To all my family and friends, who provide me with unending inspiration (though I fully maintain that any similarities are purely coincidental), I love all of you with all my heart.

Finally, thank you to everyone who read this book, especially those of you who don't know me at all, but are still taking the time to read this paragraph! ✿

ReGina Welling

From the author:

Thank you to my daughter, my heart, my co-author. This was fun, let's do it again! A bunch.

Thank you to Alan for putting up with my weird schedule and inattention when the muse is on me.

Thank you to my family and my hometown for providing a certain amount of fodder for this story.

Thank you to Peggy for making our words more sensible.

Hugs to you all! ✿

Contents

Prologue

When the rickety stepladder swayed to the left, Luther Plunkett hung on for dear life and muttered a string of words completely inappropriate for use inside a church. Momentary panic revved his pulse to pounding until the twenty-year-old wreck righted itself and he breathed a sigh of relief.

A section of trim around one of the rafters arching up into the cathedral ceiling had loosened enough to be in danger of falling onto the congregation. It was one of the many repairs on his list— and the only one that would necessitate climbing up onto the twelve-foot stepladder that had probably been around when dinosaurs roamed the earth. From this lofty height, everything looked different—smaller and more dangerous. The thought of taking a header onto those pews turned Luther's blood to ice in his veins.

Still, two rungs above the recommended climbing limit, Luther traded a certain amount of hubris for common sense: this wasn't his first day on the job and no matter what anyone said, he knew his way around the tools of his trade. Only half of his attention was focused on the repairs at hand, while the other half fumed and fretted over the way his brother, Evan, had railroaded him into taking on this job—at almost nothing over cost, no less.

How was he supposed to earn a decent living as a handyman if he didn't make a profit? That brother of his had no clue. Two or three good real estate commissions a year and Evan was rolling in the dough, leaving Luther to squirm in the dust.

Deeply absorbed in resentful thoughts and seething anger, Luther never heard the hushed feet padding toward the ladder. He felt the jolting shove, though, and felt the ladder begin to rock.

The world around him went hard and bright with fear while the ladder swayed first to the right, then back to the left. Luther scrambled down a couple of rungs and leaned against the motion to try and settle it back on a solid footing, but the force of his rushed movements only increased the pendulum-like swing. When the right hand feet lifted off the floor and the ladder passed the point of no return, Luther's heart skipped a beat and almost before it began to hammer in his chest again, the floor hurtled up to meet him.

Chapter 1

Two days earlier.

Douchebag.

The word scrawled across Chloe's notebook made Emmalina Valentina Torrence—EV to her friends—snort out loud. Mostly because, while inelegant and downright crass, it perfectly described the annoying man currently speaking to the sizable group of citizens attending the Ponderosa Pines quarterly town meeting.

A typical New England town meeting takes place once a year, but in Ponderosa Pines, anything worth doing once was worth doing four times; hence, the quarterly town meeting. Once a year, the town voted in a new set of officials; the other three meetings were less well-attended, and most often no more than a formality. Tonight, however, the mere formality had already ended and a three ring circus was about to begin. EV could tell because they'd already brought in the clown.

After fifteen minutes of fidgeting in his seat and clearing his throat repeatedly, local handyman Luther Plunkett now held court at the front of the room. Still in his work clothes, with an attempt at an earnest expression pasted on his round, freckled face and a liberal sprinkling of sawdust in his curly, mouse-brown hair, he stalked back and forth while making his plea.

"You got my hands tied with all these regulations: recycled materials, energy efficient building. That's not the way they do things in Warren or in Gilmore. I'm a business man; I gotta be able to make a profit. You all know me. I been good to my customers: always going above and beyond, but I'm losing money on every job," his voice rose to a whining pitch that grated EV's nerves and clenched her teeth.

What a phony; and worse, he was a phony with aspirations. More than anything, Luther wanted to elevate himself from a lowly handyman to a high-end contractor. Never mind that Ponderosa Pines had neither the population nor the commercial base to support such a desire.

"Bull puckey!" someone called out from the back of the room. "Why don't you shut up and sit down, Luther?" EV craned her head around to search unsuccessfully through the crowd for the heckler.

Luther's reputation for bragging about his abilities then providing shoddy construction had not stopped people hiring him. Without scrupulous supervision, Luther rushed around doing things to make himself look busy, while supplying homeowners with hurried, slapdash workmanship—for which he charged premium prices. His reputation was that of a greedy shyster with minimal skills and a big mouth.

Rising to her feet, EV moved toward the front of the hall, controlled fury giving her the grace of a panther stalking its prey. Tension announced itself in the clench of her fists, the way her eyes narrowed and cooled, the angle of her chin. Long legs carried her forward until she stood toe to toe with Luther. She had six inches of height on him, and the authority of age combined with conviction sat well on her strong shoulders.

"Reducing our carbon footprint is part of the town charter, and that means building and maintaining energy efficient homes; but it also means using a percentage of recycled materials. You're

8

asking us to set aside our goals and regulations, not for the sake of the community, but so you can increase your profit margin?" EV's voice fell like a rain of dry desert sand. She turned direct, brown eyes toward the crowd and brushed an errant strand of hair behind her ear.

Before Luther could answer, John Peterson spoke up, "Maybe you could explain why using reclaimed materials is so much harder on your bottom line. I know my cousin in Warren paid you enough to cover your crew plus exorbitant dump fees for tearing down that old barn of his. You ended up with a load of perfectly good lumber, enough usable steel roofing to do a house, and made a little profit on the job. You got a lot of nerve standing here complaining."

"Give the man a break." Evan Plunkett spoke up. No surprise there, the Plunkett brothers were cut from the same cloth. "All this green living stuff is a pipe dream. It's time to wake up and smell the coffee," he sneered. "Or would that be the Chai tea?"

Where Luther was ineptly incompetent, his younger brother Evan intentionally caused chaos. Driven by greed and a need for validation, he spent an inordinate amount of time scheming to gain a measure of control in town affairs. As careful as he tried to be, bits and pieces of his plans always made their way back to the town gossip mongers, who could disseminate information faster than the speed of light.

Such were the workings of the Ponderosa Pines grapevine. With roots running deep and true, its leafy goodness snaked through nearly every household in town before returning to the spot where its seed had long ago been planted: smack dab in the middle of EV's front yard.

If a gnat sneezed in the woods, EV knew about it. Anyone with a lick of sense would have picked another chicken to pluck, another fish to try and fry. It was a lesson both Evan and Luther seemed unable to learn.

So, when Luther offered the first selectman a cheap bathroom remodel if he voted in Evan's favor—EV knew.

When Evan got one of the survey companies he worked with in Gilmore to lay to rest a property dispute between the third selectman and her neighbor—and for once and all prove who was responsible for the dead tree neither wanted to pay to cut down—EV knew.

In the end, it had been Evan who left that meeting with his tail tucked between his legs. Thinking he had two of the town's three selectmen tucked tightly in his pocket, it was with shock and awe that he watched as the man who was supposed to slash and burn the forest, slashed and burned any chance for a vote in his favor.

Ever since then, EV had been waiting and watching for the pair of brothers to make their next move. Tonight, there was little doubt Luther's seemingly benign plea was the opening salvo to a new scheme.

Whether she wanted to admit it or not, at the tender age of thirty-three, EV had become the town matriarch and now, twenty years later, she was more firmly cast in the role than ever. Ponderosa Pines, a once thriving commune, had become next best thing to a ghost town after its founders and primary owners, EV's parents, returned to their mainstream life.

Determined to save her beloved home, EV rallied the remaining residents into expanding into a planned community with the goal of becoming an eco-friendly town. Bit by bit, year by year, with the help of those remaining members, now known as the town elders, EV brought the spirit of her parent's vision into the new age.

The only thing EV and the elders hadn't counted on was that some of the next generation might not look upon Ponderosa Pines as the paradise they all considered it to be. This was the case with Evan and Luther, whose mother—herself an elder—had not passed on her love of green living and community spirit to her sons.

Following the path from changing the town's building codes to allow for the use of shoddier, mass produced materials to its end where the door would now open for Luther to build houses on spec—houses that Evan, in his capacity as a real estate broker, could sell—was one route that needed neither a map nor a flashlight.

The whole setup was a smokescreen, EV thought as she watched the proposal get voted down. She would have bet her life on that fact. The only thing left to do was wait for the other shoe to drop.

* * *

Chloe LaRue maintained an appearance of casual interest while her keen eyes roamed around the room and observed her small community voice their opinions on Luther's proposal. Her job as gossip columnist for the *Pine Cone*, Ponderosa Pines' weekly newsletter, demanded attention to detail. 'Babble & Spin' was by far the most popular regular article, and had been since the very first issue rolled off a second-hand printing press over thirty years ago.

Too bad she couldn't take any public credit for her work; Chloe was simply the latest in a series of anonymous authors. No past writer had ever been unmasked, and Chloe wasn't about to be the first. Readers enjoyed speculating on the identity of the mystery author almost as much as they enjoyed learning scandalous information about their neighbors. Ponderosa Pines was, like most small towns, full of busybodies.

EV, as the only person Chloe ever confided in, enjoyed being privy to yet another Ponderosa secret and took great delight in helping Chloe maintain her anonymity. The fount of information stored in EV's exceptional brain was a most welcome benefit, and Chloe relied heavily on those tidbits at the beginning of her tenure at the *Cone*.

Now, as she listened to Luther continue to blather incoherently, one thought replayed in Chloe's mind:

11

I did not come back here only to watch the integrity of the community be lambasted by these two morons. And I won't let it happen without a fight.

* * *

Double douchebag.

Chloe underlined the indictment with a series of vicious pen slashes while EV muttered epithets under her breath until her patience snapped like a rubber band in sub-zero weather.

"To that intent and purpose, the town of Gilmore has expressed their agreement for the purpose of annotating…"

"Annexing." Evan hissed too loudly for a whisper.

"Annexing," Luther parroted, "the town of Ponderosa Pines."

And there it was; EV heard the echoing thump as the other shoe hit the floor. This was what the boob brothers had been leading up to all along: an attempt to combine Ponderosa Pines with neighboring Gilmore.

A mental click followed the thump.

This must be their end game; what Evan and Luther had been working toward all along. Forehead wrinkled into furrows of frown lines, EV ran through the probabilities for why now, at the very first fiscal meeting of the year—the meeting where electing new town officials had just effectively removed anyone already allied with Evan from office—would the Plunkett brothers have raised this particular issue.

Desperation had to be driving Evan. Why else would he reveal his final desire now?

"…an unparalleled opportunity to expand into the new milieu." Luther intoned as though he had been coached on what to say.

"You mean *millennium* you idiot. If you're going to try putting one over on the community, at least have the decency to use the correct terminology," EV spit the words at him.

"Oh, come on, people. Get a clue here," a voice rose above the rumbling crowd. "This is the best idea I've heard in years. Let Gilmore take over the whole damn town," Allegra Worth, who bore a striking resemblance to Cruella DeVille, declared at a higher volume than Chloe had ever heard her use before.

When she opened her mouth to add more to the comment, Allegra's husband Ashton pinned her with a glare. Undeterred, she opened her mouth to make another comment, but was stopped by her husband rising to his feet and pulling her along with him. At first she stood her ground; but, after another pointed look, she fell into line and followed him out.

Evan puffed up at the vote of confidence until EV turned her attention on him. "I know you're the one behind this. You have an ulterior motive somewhere at the heart of this ridiculous scheme, but I'm telling you now it's not going to happen."

"I only want what's best for everyone. Expansion is growth. Don't you want Ponderosa Pines to be the best it can be? To bring jobs to your neighbors? To increase the tax base?"

"And you seriously think letting Gilmore annex our town is the way to do that?" She turned to the rest of the seated residents. "Do you understand what he is asking? Are you all aware Evan ran for mayor in Gilmore and lost before moving back to Ponderosa Pines? Now, all of a sudden he wants the two towns to become one; and you can be sure that Gilmore, being the bigger town, would insist we go with their form of local government." That statement elicited a collective grumble. Ponderosa Pines was proud of its Selectman system.

"Think about it. Each and every one of you would lose your voice in town decisions unless one of our own became mayor. Evan has already expressed an interest in the job. He's betting with all of us behind him, next time, he'll be elected."

"That's rich coming from you." Evan sneered, "Face it EV; your mind went there that fast." He snapped his fingers. "Because you're just trying to protect your own interests. It isn't enough for you to own more land than anyone else in town, you have to be in control of everyone, too."

"No, Evan, that's your agenda, not mine." EV turned to address her neighbors and friends, "You all know me. I speak my mind but I have no interest in running the town. I've never accepted a nomination to any office. Ponderosa Pines may not be perfect; but as a community, we've always worked together and we always will. What possible good could come from losing our town status? Ask yourselves what Evan and Luther stand to gain."

Nods of agreement showed her words had struck home.

"Now that the proposal is on the table, we have to see it through; but I urge you to think long and hard about whose interests you are supporting before you make any decisions. Our streets have always been safe; our crime rates the lowest in the state. Will putting Gilmore, and possibly him," she pointed at Evan, "in charge keep them that way? Or will it line his and Luther's pockets at the expense of our children's safety?"

With a pointed look that Chloe easily interpreted as, "Stay, observe, and report back to me later," EV strode from the room.

* * *

Dead silence descended on the meeting in the first moments after EV's departure, then erupted into a dull roar as several townspeople left the Grange Hall. Those remaining broke into smaller groups, each trying to talk over the next. Amid the increasing noise, the town elders tried to help the three newly-appointed selectmen regain control by shouting for order.

Under normal conditions, the opinions of the elders, the very first Ponderosa Pines residents, carried authority—but tonight their voices dropped unheard into the din.

Chloe seized the opportunity to eavesdrop discretely and began to assess the room for the most interesting candidates.

Millie Jacobs and Summer Beckett lounged against a wall near the door to the hall's kitchen, heads bent together and snickering. Chloe wouldn't get any useful information out of either one of those airheads. They undoubtedly had already decided they wanted the opposite of whatever EV wanted for the community.

Jealous mean girls, that's what you are. And you're way too old for that crap. Chloe spat silently in their general direction while pasting a convincing fake smile on her face.

Not that EV had ever noticed, but Millie and Summer harbored a mutual grudge against Chloe's closest friend just because each of their husbands had been colossally stupid enough to admit they found EV attractive. EV was the kind of women men noticed. With no idea of the undercurrent, EV had been nothing but nice to these women—had no idea they bore malice toward her since she had never laid eyes on either man in an inappropriate manner. Being a desirable woman didn't make her a man stealer.

Noticing that the initial furor had finally died down, Chloe continued her evaluation of the room. A tall, muscular man wearing a rather impressive Fu Manchu mustache stood chatting with an older lady sporting knitted garments in varying colors. From the bright red beret perched jauntily on top of her head to the lime green and hot pink chevron print purse hanging from her shoulder, and with her beak-like nose, Priscilla Lewellyn looked, for all the world, like a tie-dyed chicken.

Fu Manchu's name was Horis, and Chloe wondered for the millionth time if he was hoping the elaborate mustache would draw attention away from the way his bottle-bottom glasses magnified his eyes and his unfortunate given name. Oh, what she wouldn't do to give this man a total makeover. Poor guy didn't realize there was no such thing as "dress overalls", or that he was actually a decent catch underneath the dorky exterior.

Horis was a farmer and a leader of the group of volunteers responsible for planning and organizing the community's many gardens. He was also a sweet, soft-spoken man who loved Ponderosa Pines and would presumably fight to keep Evan from rising to power. Priscilla was pleasant but eccentric; and, while Chloe thought she would side with EV, something about the woman's fluttery nature made her hard to read.

Weaving through the small crowd avoiding eye contact and putting out the I'm-not-here vibe, Chloe lingered near the pair until she caught enough of their conversation to conclude that neither would favor Evan as mayor. Nothing to worry about here.

As she peered across the room, she noticed a couple around her age who were fairly new to the community: David and Rhonda Erickson, she believed were their names. Both nondescript in appearance, they seemed like nice people who, judging by the protrusion from Rhonda's midsection, would become a family of three within the next six or seven months.

I'll keep quiet about that, Chloe thought, *don't want to put my foot in my mouth in case Rhonda's just been sampling too many whoopie pies from The Mudbucket.*

David's arms were wrapped around Rhonda's shoulders, his head bent toward hers with a worried expression on his face. They were so deep in conversation they didn't notice as Chloe slowly made her way close enough to catch a few snippets.

"That woman seems like she cares, David. We moved here to get away from the materialistic world, not have to deal with some dictatorial mayor."

"He's the one who sold us on this town in the first place. We could tell he cared about it. Now, because of the words of one whacked-out hippie chick we're going to crucify him?"

"That 'whacked-out hippie chick' was behind the grant that helped us buy the coffee shop." Rhonda's eyes flashed heat.

16

"How did you find that out? I thought the grant came from the town."

"That woman *is* the town. She might gloss over it, and from what I can tell, she's very low key about it—well, except for maybe tonight—but every good thing that has been built here, she's had a hand in. Evan may have talked up the town but it was to make the sale. I could tell that from the beginning." Something about him had given Rhonda the tingle since the first time she'd heard his smooth voice on the phone.

"Don't you think we'd get more business if we were technically located in Gilmore?"

Rhonda cocked her head and stared at her husband. "How do you think? Is there some invisible wall between here and Gilmore that would come down once the two towns combine? Don't you think it's more likely our taxes would increase and we'd have a bunch of new regulations to follow?" Rhonda was the more business-minded of the two but David was an artist in the kitchen.

"All I'm saying is, let's learn as much as we can about both of them before we take sides. We have more here to think about than just us." Rhonda confirmed Chloe's theory about her waistline.

As usual, the two 'weird sisters'—who were neither weird, nor sisters, according to EV—watched with great interest but said nothing. So rarely did they speak up at a town event, Chloe wasn't sure she had ever heard either of their voices. Their reputation for being witches was also something she had yet to confirm. EV said they were, but Chloe had her doubts. They would follow EV, though.

Having learned enough to see the majority supported the town remaining a singular entity, Chloe left the hall and headed home for some much-needed rest.

17

Chapter 2

As she ambled down the tree-lined path that led away from the portion of Ponderosa Pines that could be considered "downtown" and headed in the general direction of her house, Chloe met the daily mindfulness goal she set for herself. Each day since she moved back home she tried to take at least a few moments to feel present in her body and appreciate her surroundings.

After traveling for so long, even beautiful, majestic scenery seemed commonplace to the extent that Chloe no longer paid attention to the world around her. Tunnel vision threatened to infect other areas of her life negatively affecting her overall well-being. Focusing solely on completing the myriad of tasks required of her each day, while ignoring secondary needs and desires, took its toll. When she realized she felt trapped in her own life and body, Chloe decided it was time for a major change.

Coming back to the Pines, finding home again, was the first step in shrugging off the been-there-done-that rut she had fallen into.

Tonight, Chloe's one mindful thought was merely how beautiful the town of Ponderosa Pines had become. The community, named for the trees it was nestled among, committed itself to live gently on the land, to work with rather than against the ecology. Willing residents kept once-dense forest cleaned and thinned to make room for natural paths running throughout the town.

This section of the woods, her favorite, was frequently traveled. Twinkly lights festooned the path leading to a decorated area appropriately deemed "The Fairy Garden". Fairies of all sizes, shapes, and artistic media peeked out from beneath rocks or from their perches inside hollowed trunks and hung shimmering from every third or fourth tree limb Chloe passed. Each Ponderosa resident had contributed a fairy or two to the garden over the years—at least every resident except Chloe.

She was saving her fairy for the moment when she finally stopped holding herself back—when she let go of always being an outsider and finally embraced her place in the Pines. Years of being "the new girl" at school segued seamlessly into becoming "the new girl" at work while Chloe moved from job to job to job looking for fulfillment that never came.

Ponderosa Pines had accepted Chloe; it was just that kind of place. The fact that she was a member of one of the founding families cinched the deal. But being accepted was different from feeling fully at home, and that was something Chloe had struggled with for most of her life.

Was the restless urge to run hereditary? Her mom certainly had it in spades: and for Lila it was a case of always running toward the next exciting adventure, whereas Chloe's desperate urge often carried the flavor of running away.

No more.

Something about this place had woven through her subconscious, whispered in the corners of her mind, called her back with the promise of home.

Now it was time to see if that promise was real, or if it was just a mirage.

At the edge of the wooded path Chloe emerged into full moonlight and veered toward where her home sat in the oldest part of town. The mindful hike had worked its magic, putting her into a state of hyper focus which she used to contemplate the meeting she had just attended.

Would the community come together the way they always had in the past? Could she trust them to make the right decision or would it be time to pack it in and move on? Even if she hadn't trusted EV as implicitly as she did, it was apparent to Chloe that combining with Gilmore would change the Pines completely. Gone would be the stress on equality, teamwork, and freedom of choice that had always been in keeping with her family's ideal of what the community should be.

Approaching her house, warm lamplight shining through the windows, it looked like a painting in the deepening twilight. Chloe couldn't hold back a smile. Dwarfed by the spreading branches of a huge Sugar Maple tree, the cottage home was unobtrusive and cozy, and Chloe didn't regret a day spent in her personal paradise.

Once her mother had accepted her daughter's desperate desire to go home, she had gifted Chloe with the deed. Though she had never lived here full time before, it was the only place Chloe remembered returning to during the years when Lila had carted her around the world like a knapsack. She was grateful for those experiences, but was happier here than she had been at any other point in her life.

Chloe's grandparents built what started as a simple cabin, barely finishing it before her mother was born. They were happy here for several years while the commune rose up around them. Primarily constructed out of cordwood, a cheap and popular medium used extensively throughout the community, the main house exterior resembled mosaic tile. Stacking cross-sections of whole and split logs and cementing them into place created two-foot-thick walls that both decorated and insulated the building. Assorted pieces of beach glass, stone, and tile were set into the cement between the logs to create even more artistic interest.

Her favorite touch held a place of honor above the front door; a single log, two feet in diameter with a natural heart shaped pattern in its center. Its mate took center stage above EV's door, both having been cut and placed at the same time by Chloe's grandfather and EV's father.

EV, hearing a slew of unexpected curse words coming from Chloe's backyard about a month after she had moved in, investigated and found Chloe nearly into a pile of cut evening primrose she had mistaken for a weed. Looking around the yard EV realized that Chloe had bitten off a bit more than she could chew, pulled her inside and brewed them both a pot of tea.

Together they brought the garden back to life while forming an unbreakable friendship. Chloe loved to sit in the screen house and survey her little corner of the world. Stone paths curled around dozens of patches of earth containing a plethora of garden art and several hidden places Chloe visited to practice yoga.

Her Gramps had spent a year with knives, gouges, and chisels to carve a Celtic cross into the arched-top front door that Chloe had religiously locked every day until EV chided her. This was not the city; this was a safe place where neighbors worked together, played together and looked out for one another. There was always a helping hand at the ready, and Chloe knew she could knock on any door and receive assistance if she ever needed it.

"Nothing bad ever happens in Ponderosa Pines" was the town mantra. It drifted through her head and quieted her thoughts as she readied for bed. Chloe relished the notion as she floated off to sleep to the sounds of chirping crickets and croaking tree frogs.

Chapter 3

When EV had stalked down the same path half an hour ahead of Chloe, meditative walking had been the farthest thing from her mind. She stomped through the fairy garden barely resisting the urge to kick one of the winged creations to kingdom come. It would feel so good.

In another forty-five minutes, an hour at the most, the Ponderosa Pines gossip mill would start to kick into full grinding mode. Before that happened, EV needed time to think about the possible repercussions from tonight's meeting.

Her long legs ate the hike through the woods like a dieter gulping down a midnight binge. Once home, she circled her living room with the frustrated energy of a caged tiger until it became clear pacing wasn't enough to provide release. Glancing at her watch to gauge how far along she was in the countdown to gossip liftoff, EV took the stairs to her bedroom two at a time.

After yanking a tank top and yoga pants onto her lanky frame, she smoothed her hair into a stubby tail at the back of her head. Chloe's yoga might be the commune-approved method of stress relief, but EV preferred beating the living crap out of something. To that end, she had installed a punching bag in the far end of her bedroom.

No gloves tonight. Only the force of bare skin against firm leather would do.

Ten minutes later, coated in a light sheen of sweat, she was lost to the rhythm—jab, jab, kick, jab, kick. She pummeled the bag into submission until her entire body hummed into a zen state.

Tomorrow's bruises would serve as a reminder that letting Evan goad her this deeply into the red had given him power over her.

When the special ring tone that signaled a text from Chloe sounded, EV heaved a sigh and flicked the touchscreen to open her message folder.

Common sense rules, douchebag drools—Mata Hari

A second text shot into her inbox.

Looks like he mostly got the bobble-heads and Cruella so far. Maybe one or two others and the fence sitters are minimal.

Thumbs flying, EV typed a reply.

I'll be tending the grapevine the rest of the evening.

I think this is going to die down without much of a fuss. Chloe might be right, but EV suspected the fuss was just beginning.

Don't put money on it.

To EV's way of thinking, politics and deer ticks were not that far different. They both carried the kind of disease that could make life a living hell; the only difference was that deer ticks were more easily avoided and you could pick them off with just a little tug while politics dug in deeper.

Her blood pressure had just settled back into the normal range when the phone pealed with the first call of the night. It was well past the witching hour when she finally fell into bed.

Chapter 4

Chloe finished dabbing her lips with a bit of fruity gloss and stepped back to assess her reflection in the mirror. Blond hair fell in waves around a pretty, heart-shaped face and almond-colored eyes. Hours spent outdoors had given her natural highlights that would have cost a fortune at any decent salon and a smattering of light freckles across her petite but slightly upturned nose.

The last time Chloe dolled herself up was months ago, but an impending night out had her dressed to the nines. She wore a pair of teal and bright blue color-blocked (and surprisingly comfortable) wedges; a white, fitted maxi skirt with blue stitching; and a flowing teal tank top that showed off just enough cleavage.

Just before leaving the bathroom, Chloe gave her hair one last fluff and then checked to make sure her underwear wasn't showing through her skirt. That would be embarrassing.

The girls were due any minute now, and Chloe was excited for an evening that didn't consist of sifting through gossip and contemplating conspiracy theories. She and her friends had only seen each other in passing lately and hadn't all been together at the same time for weeks. An evening of fun was definitely in order, and she was guaranteed a good time whenever Veronica and Mindy were involved.

She heard the doorbell ring and yelled from the hallway "get your asses in here already; you know the doorbell is for losers!" Bounding to the foyer she flung the door open and came face to face with Nathaniel Harper, the last person she would have expected.

"So that's an open invitation then, huh?" he asked, wiggling his eyebrows suggestively.

Chloe put a hand on her hip and stuck her tongue out at Nate before reaching up to hug her oldest childhood friend.

"When did you get back?" she exclaimed as she ushered him into her living room. The stack of blue, white, and teal bangle bracelets jangled on her wrist as Chloe handed Nate a glass of the red wine she had been aerating for her friends.

"Late last night."

"And what brings you back to our itty bitty town? I thought you were some hotshot detective in the city. Or has your mother blown your accomplishments out of proportion?" Chloe fiddled with the rhinestone-studded pendant that hung around her neck.

Everyone knew Barbara Harper thought the sun rose and set on her son, but they also knew it was with good reason since Nathaniel had always flown the straight and narrow and deserved all the accolades he received.

"Apparently hot shot detectives aren't immune to injury. I damaged my rotator cuff swinging off a fire escape to catch a suspect and had to have surgery. I've got another month of therapy and I hate desk duty so my boss sent me here to keep an eye on his newest deputy and 'get back to my roots'. Ask me how thrilled I am."

Nate rose from the couch and wandered into the kitchen. She knew precisely what he was looking for, and when he returned holding a giant no-bake cookie Chloe couldn't help but smile. She had reorganized cabinets and closets, replaced several pieces of furniture and added her own flair to the decor, but one thing she

26

couldn't bring herself to change was the location of her Nana's goody cabinet.

Though she claimed keeping the old orange and white Tupperware container stocked with what Nana had called "brown cookies" was a gesture meant to satisfy the children who frequently ran rampant through her home, there was more to it than that. Each time she repeated the old ritual of boiling butter, sugar, and chocolate over medium heat, then adding peanut butter and oatmeal and pouring the batter onto waxed paper Chloe was carrying on a beloved tradition.

It warmed her heart to know Nate also remembered the treats, and that he felt comfortable enough in her home to nip one without asking. It also warmed her heart to know that he'd be sticking around for a while.

"Well I, for one, am glad you're back."

* * *

This time there was no doorbell, just the sound of Chloe's girlfriends chattering as they pushed through the front door, picked up a glass of wine each, and deposited themselves on her couch.

Chloe's two best friends could not have differed more in both appearance and personality.

Mindy, a lively redhead whose petite stature and ever-so-slightly pointed ears gave her an elf-like quality, had been dating the same guy practically since middle school. Neither had any desire to get married or have kids—a point of view that was not out of place in a community where many couples had never officially tied the knot, or had been bound by ritual handfasting in place of a traditional wedding ceremony.

Veronica, on the other hand, was a striking brunette with a husband and a current total of five children. All that childbearing had only enhanced her voluptuous shape, making it the epitome of an hourglass figure and the subject of much envy from the less fortunate women of Ponderosa Pines. Her somewhat dippy nature belied a level of intelligence that continually surprised and pleased her closest friends.

You could have a highly sophisticated philosophical discussion with Veronica one minute, then spend the next hour convincing her the large bird she saw flying around was definitely not a pterodactyl. This was her monthly kid-free outing; it was unusual to see her without a child attached to her hip.

That left Chloe as the only one of the three not in a committed relationship, and she was okay with that for the time being. She loved Veronica's kids like nieces and nephews, but enjoyed being able to hand them back at the end of the day.

"Was that Nathaniel Harper I just saw coming out of your house? When did Mr. Hottie get back to town?" Veronica asked. Chloe could tell she was practically drooling. It was true that Nathaniel was a good looking man. Everyone but Chloe saw a tall, muscular physique; blue eyes coated in thick, black lashes; and wavy chestnut hair that curled just around his temples. But to her he was still a small child giving her wet willies when she least expected, and an awkward teenager growing into lanky limbs and protruding ears.

Every few years when Lila and Chloe would visit the Pines, she and Nate would fall back into a natural friendship. They even tried making out once during high school, but it hadn't ended well. She didn't remember who started laughing first.

"Last night, and he's not planning on leaving anytime soon, either." Chloe filled Veronica and Mindy in on Nate's new position with the police department.

"You sure you don't want a piece of that, Chlo?" asked Mindy with a suggestive raise of her brow, "I'm sure he'd happily put you in cuffs anytime you're up for it."

Veronica and Mindy both knew Chloe had no interest in Nate, but they also loved poking fun at her perpetual single status and weren't going to give up until she had hooked up.

"Let it go, and let's get going before we miss all the fun." Chloe practically pulled them out the door and into the car.

* * *

Ten minutes later, singing a Cyndi Lauper song loudly and off key, Chloe pulled into the neon-splashed parking lot of the Barnyard, a favorite Gilmore hangout, and they all piled out of her battered Mini Cooper. The Barnyard was aptly named. Once a falling down wreck, the nearly hundred-year-old barn had been rehabilitated and turned into an entertainment center for adults who wanted to act like children—which meant the place was always busy and always a good time.

A circular bar occupied the center of the enormous barn, surrounded by high-top tables and mismatched bar stools. The front right corner of the room held a vintage arcade complete with games like Super Mario Bros, Centipede, and Skeeball. The other corner boasted several pool tables and dart boards, a few booths, and a number of flat screen TVs playing everything from sports to old movies and 80's MTV videos.

The entire back of the barn was reserved for dancing, live music, and karaoke. Mismatched tile formed a patchwork patterned dance floor and helped maintain the comfortable, homey vibe that encouraged customers to stay late and drink profusely. Photo booths scattered throughout the bar streamed pictures onto a big screen mounted above the dance floor so that everyone could see just how silly you were acting behind the curtains.

After carefully surveying the room Chloe, Veronica, and Mindy headed for an unoccupied booth in the pool and dart room, which also just happened to be filled with a variety of attractive male specimens. While Chloe was the only one who could reap those particular benefits, Veronica and Mindy never turned down a chance to objectify the opposite sex. They were both on the prowl to find a date for their friend and began pointing out possibilities before ordering the first round of drinks.

"Cowboy Boots over there would definitely do in a pinch." Mindy nodded toward a man in tight-fitting jeans and a flannel shirt while absently accepting a vodka soda with lime from their waitress.

"Eh, not really my thing. I'm more a t-shirt and flip-flops kind of girl. Preferably a tight t-shirt bursting with arm muscles, but cowboy boots just always look a little girly to me."

"What about Socks & Sandals by the dart board in the corner?" Veronica asked with a sly grin. "What situation do you suppose he's preparing for where he needs both?"

"Ooh, ooh, I spotted the hipsters!" Mindy exclaimed, pointing toward a table of guys in their late 20's who were obviously members of one of the more obnoxious social groups to have emerged lately. From the tops of their fedora-adorned Bieber-cut heads to their custom-designed Converse sneakers, everything about them irritated Chloe to no end.

"You're not a lumberjack; you don't hunt to survive; and every time I see you, you're drinking a craft beer or a mocha-choca-frappa-latte with extra foam. Therefore, you did not earn and do not deserve that beard you're sporting! Beards and skinny jeans, brilliant combination." she ranted in their general direction.

"OK, forget the hipsters; you know what a trigger they are for Chloe" Veronica admonished Mindy with a mischievous grin.

Chloe looked around at the men in the room, trying to imagine herself approaching someone with the intent of making a romantic connection. It had been quite a while since her last relationship; traveling had taken its toll, and she had never been one for long term commitments.

Most men were intimidated by her independence, and allowing work to rule her life had left little room for anyone or anything else. She had been on one or two dates since returning to Ponderosa Pines, but had learned rather quickly that privacy in this town was harder to come by than a two-dollar bill.

Just because she hadn't liked when Rosalina Emmons' son had taken her to a "nice dinner" at the Snack Shack, or that all Shane Davis wanted to talk about was the pot plants he was trying to grow in the field behind the cow pasture didn't mean she was a snob who was too good for everyone in town.

Enough had been enough when she had heard someone she barely knew discussing the awkward kiss the latter had tried to land on her at the end of the night. Nope, she would no longer be accepting dates with anyone who lived in the Pines. Unfortunately, since she rarely left the little hamlet anymore, her chances of meeting anyone had diminished to the point where she had decided there was a chance she would wind up an old lady with 57 cats.

"Hey, isn't that Talia Plunkett over there dancing like it's 1999?" Mindy pointed not at all inconspicuously at the wife of the man Chloe and EV unaffectionately referred to as Douchebag #2. Luther didn't deserve the title of number one; he lacked the faculties necessary to be taken seriously in any capacity.

His wife, on the other hand, was a horse of a different color. Far more desirable than Luther, it was a mystery to many—and to Talia's sister Lottie in particular—how the pair had come together in the first place. Lottie hated Luther, partly because she was insanely jealous that her younger sister, Talia, married before she did.

Peering past Talia's vibrating backside, Chloe observed Luther's dancing skills, and once again came down on Lottie's side in her estimation of the couple. Talia seemed to be enjoying herself thoroughly. *To each their own,* Chloe thought.

Veronica, ignoring the fact that the woman was clearly drunk and attempting to perform a sexy number that was coming off more like the chicken dance, zeroed in on what she considered most important about the scene: fashion. "I know Luther jacks prices a bit, but do you suppose he really has enough money for her

31

to be spending hundreds of dollars on a scarf? That's vintage Pucci, if I'm not mistaken. It must have cost a pretty penny."

Raising five kids left little cash for luxuries like expensive accessories, but Veronica was still a fiend. She bargain shopped and mixed vintage finds with cheap knockoffs, always managing to look chic and original. Trusting that Veronica knew her Pucci, Chloe filed the comment away in the back of her mind for later contemplation.

"Time for a trip to the Ladies, ladies. Anyone need a touch up?" Mindy led them on a winding path toward the restrooms and through saloon doors labeled "Cowgirls". The line stretched almost back to the door, and Chloe kept one ear perked for gossip; she couldn't allow any prime opportunity for column fodder to go unchecked—no matter how much she had wanted a night away. If a Pines resident was mentioned within earshot, Chloe was going to do her best to *accidentally* overhear anything that might prove useful.

Snaking around the corner and into a section of restroom lined with three stalls, Chloe and her friends overheard a familiar name as the two women occupying the stalls carried on what they couldn't have possibly thought was a private conversation. *Jackpot.*

"…Evan, that guy who ran for mayor. He tried to get me to go on a date with him, telling me he was 'setting himself up to be the most powerful man in Gilmore' and that I should 'hop on board the Evan train while I had the chance.'" Chloe rolled her eyes at the last comment, while Mindy stifled an hysterical giggle.

"Well, *I* heard he's got a clandestine affair going on with some woman in that sorry excuse for a town. He'll never get into office with a scandal like that going around."

As the three women stepped out of their respective stalls almost simultaneously, Chloe and her friends shot each other looks of amusement and quietly took their places inside hoping to hear the next part of the conversation. At that moment the DJ's booming voice rose above the music and whisked away whatever words were spoken. *Interesting,* thought Chloe. *Very interesting.*

32

Chapter 5

Parked in front of the church where Luther was supposed to be working, Evan's stomach clenched then tossed up a wash of acid when he saw the now familiar handwriting scrawled across the third envelope in the pile of mail he'd tossed onto his passenger seat earlier. Whoever had his nuts in the wringer must be fully connected because it had only been two days since the town meeting, and it took at least a day to get mail here from Gilmore.

He'd failed; Evan knew that as he raked a hand through his hair with short, angry strokes until it stood uncharacteristically on end. He'd figured EV would kick up a ruckus, which was why he had tried to work around her by setting up a meeting with the selectmen first. When they hadn't gone for the plan, he saw no other choice than to lay it out at the quarterly meeting. He should have known that nothing much went on in Ponderosa Pines without her knowledge. Knocking her down a peg or two while she watched some of her iron-fisted control slip away was nearly as big a draw as getting out of the tight spot he was in.

Being blackmailed into convincing the townspeople of Ponderosa Pines to throw in and combine their town with neighboring Gilmore had not seemed like much of a hardship since it dovetailed nicely with his deepest desire: to launch a political career by becoming mayor. Total win-win, really. His mind spun out the fantasy—Ponderosa Pines citizens would jump on the opportunity to be annexed by the larger town. Then, in order to maintain some feeling of control, they would wield their voting power to slap his butt in the mayor's office where he could finally take Miss Holier Than Thou Torrence off her high horse and, as an added bonus, make the blackmail go away.

He knew high and mighty EV thought he was all about the money, but she was wrong. He had plans for Ponderosa Pines. Once he was in a position of authority, and had the blackmailer off his back, he could work toward opening up the middle of town, let in a smaller chain store or two, take some of the tax burden off the community and provide jobs.

Before it was all over, he'd be considered a genius, a benevolent benefactor even. They'd erect a statue of him in the center of town. He'd be the man who saved this godforsaken hole of a planned community from itself.

Evan was still basking in that daydream when his brother pulled up behind him. Luther slammed the pickup door, annoyance evident in the way he moved, "I was out with my wife. What's so all-fired important that you needed me to get the the church tonight?"

"I thought you were going to be working. You're going to finish here by tomorrow, right?"

"Probably not. I'd need two guys to help, but I got all the workers over in Emerson digging holes to pour footings for that addition. Can't ask them to work all day and all night, too."

Luther hefted a small stack of trim molding over one shoulder, nearly slapping his brother in the head with it as he turned to go back inside.

Clamping down on the urge to punch his own sibling, Evan merely pinched the bridge of his nose between two fingers to relieve the tension headache that threatened to settle there.

"It's not a paying job; I gotta keep my guys on the paying work or I don't make no money." The whine in Luther's tone grated on Evan's nerves.

"Then do it yourself. Just get it done by end of day tomorrow. I got another blackmail letter today, and I need as many chips as I can cash in with the board before the referendum meeting in a few days. This needs to go in my favor or I'm toast. With that witch against me, I'm screwed unless I can line up the selectmen on my side. And that's never going to happen unless you do your part."

"I still think you should just talk to her. EV's not as bad as you think. You used to like her. "

"Yeah, well, things change." Evan poked Luther in the shoulder, "Now tell me you're going to finish up here by tomorrow." It was an order.

"Only way that's going to happen is if I work all night."

"If that's what it takes…" Evan broke off when he heard the footsteps and voices of a couple out for an evening stroll. "He's got me by the short hairs. Do you need me to lay it out for you?" He left off the *again*, but it was implied in his condescending tone. His brother might be good at fibbing his way into jobs, but there was no doubt which one of them had gotten the brains in the family. Luther liked to say that his customer service skills were top notch and that it was because he knew how to talk to potential clients, that he was *articular*. Every time he heard and corrected his brother, it set Evan's teeth on edge.

What an idiot.

Still, Evan had promised his mother that he would look after his older brother. And what kind of deal was that anyway? Shouldn't it be the other way around? Shows she hadn't had much confidence in Luther's skills.

Getting him on board had been easy enough; all it had taken was a promise to loosen up on the building codes that forced Luther to use certain materials—materials that he could not mark up to make more money. It was the first step in getting rid of the

35

alternative building requirements. Then there had been the promise of more work.

Flipping his brother a piece of the commercial pie was not as much a given as Evan had led Luther to believe. There was no way he was up to the challenge of actually being a contractor on any scale, especially at the level required for what Evan had in mind. The smaller projects that he was barely qualified for would keep him busy for a couple years; and, right now, Evan needed him to be a vocal proponent for incorporating the two towns together.

What Luther also didn't know was that Evan didn't give a tiny rat's tuckus whether he helped his brother or not. Getting into office was his main focus. Increasing commercialism was just one of his plans and not even the one most likely to further his ambitions.

A career in real estate, even a lucrative one, paled in comparison to his true life's ambition of becoming a politician. It should be an easy progression from small town mayor to becoming a member of the House of Representatives and from there, to Senate or Congress.

Previously a resident of Gilmore, he had already run for mayor there each of the past three years and been summarily shut down by receiving less than one third of the vote. Not surprising since most of the residents thought Ponderosa Pines was an embarrassment. A community of aging hippies and their equally-tripped-out children couldn't hope to have produced a worthy Mayoral candidate.

The fact that other than their commitment to green living, Ponderosa Pines was very like any other town went ignored. Once a commune, always a commune—at least in the eyes of their neighbors. Unless they were able to successfully annex Ponderosa Pines and absorb it into Gilmore. Then, the added tax dollars would go a long way toward offsetting any lingering embarrassment.

Once on board with the plan, the powers that be in Gilmore all assumed the residents of Ponderosa Pines would be thankful to be taken under the wing of such a successful town. They had no idea that the scorn with which they viewed what they considered to be the *less fortunate* was returned twofold by people who valued independence and diversity.

EV having an in with the town elders—hell, she was practically one of them herself—and being unafraid to speak her mind about how she thought things should be done had not helped either. That woman was a loud-mouthed nuisance, and the fact that she and Evan's mother had been friends back in the day meant she knew every stupid childhood deed he had ever committed.

Every time she cast one of her sour looks his way, he knew she must still see him as a capricious boy. The notion that he desired her respect above all others was one that would have surprised him no end if he had ever had the self-awareness to understand or accept it.

A rustle in the bushes outside the church caught Evan's attention as he stepped through the door. He stopped to listen for a full minute, but there was not another sound. Stray cat, most likely. Even if he had felt the two pairs of eyes that were now locked on him, his courage was not up to combing the bushes so, with an uneasy feeling, he got back into his car and zoomed away.

Chapter 6

Chloe opened one eye and immediately closed it again as a thousand fireworks exploded inside her head. Her stomach curled into a fetal position and locked itself into a sailor's Alpine Butterfly knot. A loud banging that Chloe had mistaken for blood pumping through her temples was punctuated by a tinkling she recognized as the wind chime next to the front door.

Even before she heard the key turn in the lock and the door open Chloe knew her visitor must be EV. What she couldn't understand was why EV would be visiting so very early, especially after the last time she had dared disturb her friend at what Chloe considered an inappropriate hour.

For that, EV must pay.

Cracking one eyelid she turned toward her nightstand and realized it was after noon.

Whatever it is, it can wait, Chloe thought to herself while pulling a silky, monogrammed sleep mask over her eyes. The script aptly read "I'd rather be sleeping," and Chloe couldn't remember having ever agreed with the sentiment more than she did right now. She could just make out the sound of some bustling around downstairs and a tinkling of metal on glass, but chose to ignore it and instead concentrate on stopping her head from spinning.

"Morning, Miss Sleepy Pants, did you have a fun night out?" EV asked in an ear-splitting sing-song voice as she barged into Chloe's room and set a breakfast tray down on the edge of the rumpled bed.

Receiving only a grunt in response, EV tugged on the thin embroidered quilt that was covering all but Chloe's head. "I made you something to help you feel better. It's an old Torrence family hangover cure, and it works like a charm. I gave the recipe to Maggie Mullen a good ten years ago, and you can barely tell she gets hammered at least five out of seven nights a week. Come to think of it, maybe I should have kept it to myself instead of becoming an enabler."

Realizing she wasn't going to be able to shake her friend until she at least sampled the magic elixir, Chloe pushed the sleep mask onto her forehead and propped herself up against the headboard. *Relentless, as always*, Chloe mused while EV went around the room closing blinds, then turned on a small lamp in the corner. Chloe sipped the concoction that, as far as she could tell, contained orange juice, ginger, and a good dollop of hot sauce. By the time EV had settled herself in Chloe's favorite comfy reading chair the color had begun to return to her face and the room had stopped spinning like a top.

"Everything was fine until Veronica started buying tequila shots for everyone. It seemed like a good idea at the time."

"It always does, until you're praying to the porcelain god the next morning."

"At least we had the wherewithal to take a cab home. I know why you're here, by the way, and I know it's not just to nurse me back to health—although I do appreciate it. Of course I kept my eyes and ears open, at least until the end of the night. You want to know about what I happened to spy with my little eye, don't you?"

"Why I never," EV retorted in a fairly believable southern accent.

"I'm 100% convinced that the Ericksons are having a baby. They were playing some pretty hardcore darts and looked like they were enjoying themselves, but she was sipping water and I noticed him place his hand on her stomach in a fatherly way."

"They seem like a cute young couple, and it's not as though there's an excess of kids running around here save for your friend Veronica's brood. Good for them. But that was an easy one, and not exactly of the juiciest variety. What else you got?"

"Talia Plunkett was pretty drunk and should definitely never try for a dancing career. Luther was with her, and for all the world I can't figure out how the two of them wound up together."

"You and half the town. Lottie practically had an apoplectic fit when they announced their engagement. Serious case of sour grapes is the general opinion about town, but I think it's more that Lottie thought she could do better."

"By far the biggest news I got was that Luther's jerky brother has been rumored to be partaking in a scandalous affair with a married Pines resident. And also hitting on co-eds, but big shocker there. No names were mentioned, and I doubt the girls who were talking about him actually know anything anyway. But the rumor is definitely out there, and I wouldn't be surprised in the least if it was true. He's a smarmy, cocky ass; and I wouldn't put anything past him."

"Gee, Chlo, tell me how you really feel." EV snorted with a grin. "Let's tuck that little bit of information away and see if we can find out the real deal. He's going down, one way or another." She cocked an eyebrow at Chloe suggestively and changed the subject abruptly.

"You're wrong, you know. Don't you realize the very biggest reason I'm trying to resuscitate you is that I want to know if you met a man? I half hoped you wouldn't be alone when I got here."

Chloe rolled her eyes for what felt like the millionth time in response to the same question. "Why is everyone so pushy about finding me a man? Am I giving off some bitch vibe that makes you all think I need to get a piece? I'm perfectly capable of making myself happy." She paused and before EV could let a giggle escape her lips at that last comment, fixed her with a stare that clearly stated, "Now is not the time." It only lasted a moment until Chloe herself couldn't keep from smiling.

"I'm just not comfortable hooking up with someone. It's not like I'm going to form any real connection with some guy in a bar—especially not at The Yard where Objective #1 is to hook up with the first drunk girl who makes a bad decision. I'd like more than that, especially after being out of the game for so long."

She didn't mention how lonely she had been lately. That would just add fuel to EV's fire. The last thing she wanted was to be set up with every moderately attractive man EV met; and it was in her friend's nature to meddle, especially if EV thought she was helping.

EV shot an appraising look at Chloe. "And there's absolutely nobody you think you might be able to have a serious relationship with?"

"I swear, the next person who mentions the name *Nate Harper* to me is going to get a box of dirty socks for Christmas."

"Save that for the Yankee Swap this year and stop being petulant. He's good looking, has a job, and you know he's not a psychopath or a big crybaby. You could certainly do worse."

"What makes you all even think he wants anything more than friendship with me?" she asked, tentatively. If Nate had his sights set on her, she was not going to enjoy breaking his heart.

"He's not dead, Chloe, and I've seen the way he looks at you."

Chloe shifted uncomfortably and visibly reddened. "And how's that?"

"Like a ten-year-old looking at a sweaty Popsicle he'd like to lick."

Not knowing what to say, Chloe simply laid back down and closed her eyes. Was it true that she felt a spark whenever Nate was around? Maybe. Was he attractive, and someone she felt safe with? Certainly. But was Nate going to stick around long enough for a relationship? Not likely. He'd hightail it out of town faster than you could say "Boo" as soon as he could, and she wasn't about to embark on a relationship that wasn't going anywhere. She had no intention of moving, and long distance never worked out. She should know.

"Just think about it." EV left it at that, covered Chloe with a blanket and let her friend finish sleeping off the previous night. *She'll figure it out for herself.* EV thought with a chuckle.

Chapter 7

Somehow, much to the chagrin of its residents, Ponderosa Pines was slowly becoming a destination spot for the eco-curious. While tourism was not encouraged—the town was not listed in any brochures handed out at information kiosks along the highway— neither was anyone ever turned away. Curiosity was tolerated as a necessary evil and a bit of extra income.

Talia's sister Lottie owned Open House, one of two bed and breakfast establishments in town, and Sabra Pruitt ran the other, aptly named Come On Inn located directly across the road.

Both women had very different reasons for taking in lodgers. Lottie pinned her hopes of finding a husband on renting rooms to what she hoped would become a slew of eco-minded bachelors. So far, her master plan had yielded only one rather hairy, unmarried fellow who smelled as though he had developed an almost unheard of allergy to any bar of soap.

She might have been able to overlook that small detail if he hadn't been so vocally disgusted to learn people from the Pines actually owned computers and occasionally shopped at IKEA. His week-long stay ended a few days early after he commented loudly in front of Horis that no self-respecting green community member would be caught dead driving a car, using a gas-powered rototiller, or wearing clothing they had not made by hand.

Horis had deadpanned that even the Amish made their own soap before giving the young man a dunking in one of his irrigation ditches then frog-marching him off the property. The hairy complainer's Birkenstock-clad feet barely touched the ground the entire time.

Most of Lottie's customers came from politer, more considerate couples looking to learn alternative building methods and visitors drawn in during town festivals.

Sabra catered to the same crowd, but socked every penny away toward building herself a rooftop observatory where she could scan the skies for proof of alien life.

Both establishments suffered from being hard to find, hidden from the auspices of GPS by being on an unmapped, dead-end road about half a mile from the center of town.

Worse, neither woman was above poaching unregistered guests who might have mistaken one inn for the other—the two buildings being similarly constructed often confused potential guests—which only fed the rivalry between Lottie and Sabra.

Typically, EV avoided getting involved in the ongoing feud, but today it might work in her favor. Annoyed people always passed along the best gossip.

Now for the bribe.

Lifting up on her tiptoes, EV reached into the cabinet over the fridge and pulled out a jar of crab apple jelly made with her mother's secret ingredient—a squeeze of ginger juice to give it a little bite. Sabra had been trying to figure out the recipe for years. One of these days Sabra would have some gossip juicy enough to warrant being let in on the secret, but today was not that day.

The jelly went into a canvas bag along with several books that EV intended to drop off in the borrow boxes along the way.

Someone's brainchild over the years, the borrow boxes were one of EV's favorite Ponderosa Pines innovations. Perched atop a post, each box boasted a peaked roof and glass door to keep out rain and snow. In summer, the boxes contained books for trade. Townspeople were welcome to select a book as long as they replaced it with another. In winter, the boxes contained knitted hats, mittens, and scarves—no trade required. Priscilla and her knitting group stocked the boxes every couple of days.

Armed with her bag of goodies, EV stepped out into the baking heat where sweat immediately beaded on her brow. It was the kind of day where you had to make your own breeze. So instead of the leisurely stroll she had been planning, EV lifted her bike down from where it hung on a pair of hooks screwed into the ends of the logs that made up the walls of her home.

A short time later, she wheeled into Sabra's yard and prepared herself for the inevitable attack. She didn't have long to wait before the ugliest pug dog in town raced across the yard to bark at her.

"Hush up, Mugly Pugington; I'm wise to your act." The dog grinned up at her with crooked teeth poking over his top lip. Chase the Bike was his favorite game, though since he only had one good sprint in him, it never lasted long enough for him to ever catch one. Take now, for instance, he had already waddled off to fall over, panting, into the grass where he waited for EV to come give his soft, pink belly a scratch.

Having heard the barking, Sabra stepped onto the porch. She was a woman of substance and plenty of it. Salt and pepper hair flowed down her back and over a pair of watermelon-sized bosoms clad in a tank top so tight EV could see the floral pattern of her bra poking through the material. Based on other things poking through the material, the thick, rammed-earth walls of her place were doing their job and keeping the interior of her house nice and cool.

"Come in out the heat. Homemade root beer?"

"Always." Sabra's brew was like heaven in a glass: deep, dark, and rich with a scent that could make an angel sing. At the first sip from the frosted mug, foam tickled EV's nose; sighing with pleasure, she reached into her bag to pull out the jelly.

"Ooh, is that…"

"Crabapple jelly." It might have been a bribe, but EV couldn't help finding satisfaction in Sabra's obvious delight at the gift.

While the exteriors of the adjacent B&Bs were eerily similar, the interiors couldn't be more different. Stuccoed walls painted a pristine white to reflect more light was Lottie's choice for every room while, here, Sabra had chosen earthier colors like a mustard-like ocher and terra cotta for the walls to play up the variations in texture. Shelves and tables with chunky legs in dark walnut contrasted perfectly against their warm tones.

Between the banks of solar panels mounted on the roof, several skylights delivered plenty of natural light—always a concern when using extra thick walls to maintain energy efficiency. Sabra had also added a few recessed lights whose beams were directed toward the shelves that housed her bottle collection.

The woman must spend all her free time polishing glass, judging by the way each bottle sparkled in the light. Still, the jeweled colors really were beautiful additions to an already pleasing room.

"Quite the to-do the other night, eh?" As always, gossip was a give-and-take thing which meant Sabra was just as eager to get EV's opinion on recent events as EV was to get hers.

"I know, right?"

"I noticed a certain married someone watching Evan very closely during the meeting?"

"Who?" *And how did I miss that?* EV wondered.

"Ever seen a cougar on the prowl? The human variety, I mean."

EV waved a hand for Sabra to continue but knew, from way-too-satisfied look on her face, the other woman was not going to spill the details, "Let's just say the feline in question is barely out of the kitten stage, and I'm thinking he might have been willing meat."

"Evan has been known to do some prowling of his own."

"Well, there was a vibe between them, so I'm pretty sure it wasn't one-sided. Feel sorry for her husband, though. I don't think he has a clue his wife was giving some other man the side eye." Astute though she was, EV knew she had dropped the ball by being so preoccupied with trying to parse out Evan's ulterior motives she lost track of the nuances going on around her.

"What do you think about this whole Gilmore scheme?"

"Worst idea in history. No, second worst behind Evan Plunkett becoming mayor of anything. Can you just imagine? First thing he'd do is put up a statue of himself in the middle of town."

Wrinkling up her nose at the thought of that preening jackass being immortalized in stone, or worse, in bronze, EV nodded her agreement. Even with heavy campaigning, the list of people who would support Evan in his bid for office was minimal at best. Most had come here to escape forms of town government that hinged on the opinions of the few over the good of the many.

Funny, though, how some of those who, upon arrival in Ponderosa Pines, were most vocal about wanting a committee-style system; but then went completely off the deep end when that same committee decided against something they wanted. But that was only human nature, she supposed.

Mind wandering, she missed most of the story Sabra was telling about Lottie's latest lodger.

A smirk flirted across Sabra's face, "Lottie nearly had a hemorrhage," she lowered her voice conspiratorially, " if you ask me, I think her whole problem is she could use a little romp in the sheets."

Even if she agreed with Sabra on that score, EV would never admit it out loud. There was a fine line, for her, between harmless gossip and the spiteful kind. Okay, so it was a hair-thin line and moved around a lot—depending on who she was with—but still, Sabra and Lottie were rivals and agreeing with Sabra now was too much like taking sides

After being quizzed for about the hundredth time about her mother's secret jelly ingredient, EV took her leave and pedaled back to the Mudbucket for a cup of coffee and a bit of eavesdropping.

The place was nearly deserted when EV settled into her usual spot—the table in the far corner, nearest the kitchen. When young Rhonda Erickson served her an iced coffee with a double shot of caramel alongside a turkey club sandwich, EV cast a calculating eye over her figure.

Sure enough, Chloe had been right. Mrs. Erickson was expecting. If the slight thickening of her middle hadn't been enough, there was the telltale puffiness around her face and neck that often signaled a woman approaching the middle of her second trimester.

"Sit down, Rhonda. Looks like those ankles of yours could use a rest."

"But Mr. Burnsoll needs a refill."

"You sit right here and let me take care of Dalton." Before Rhonda knew what hit her, she was seated at the table, and EV was behind the counter, "decaf or regular?"

"Decaf," his grin was a mile wide as he gave her the once-over. Not in a lecherous way, but in an I-like-what-I-see kind of way. The corners of his eyes crinkled when she bristled under his gaze.

Debating whether to pour decaf in his cup or in his lap, EV snapped, "Eyes to yourself, mister." She refilled his cup.

Newly divorced—and that was a story EV intended to learn more about, though, so far, he had kept hush on the details— Dalton had used the opportunity to make more than a few new life choices. The first had been to sell this very establishment to the Ericksons. He'd recently gotten himself a new job and now, it looked as though he might be ready to start dating again.

Taller than her by a couple inches, Dalton's love of hiking kept him physically fit. Thick, dark hair curled softly at his collar with only touches of gray at the temples giving away his age. Dark eyes framed by a few crinkling laugh lines gazed at her with the barest hint of a twinkle.

He was a good looking man, a pleasant man, but totally not her type if she had a type, which she did not.

"Can't help it; you're a fine figure of a woman, Emmalina."

Now she regretted not dumping the coffee in his lap.

"EV."

"EV," his voice was a caress.

"You're not my type, Dalton. Give it a rest."

"I could be if you give me half a chance."

That this was nothing short of truth had exactly the opposite effect Dalton intended. EV froze, tension tightening her spine, setting her back teeth on edge. Before she could stop it, her imagination went on a flight of fancy; the two of them holding hands, snuggling in front of a roaring fire, growing older together. Admitting she needed or wanted any of these things set up shrieking alarms in her head. EV's mental doors slammed shut with a resounding thunk. Letting Dalton in? Worst idea in history. Admitting the possibility she might want to? Never.

"Never going to happen. I've seen you in diapers, remember?" Dalton was another second generation resident. His folks were among the few remaining original commune members, so he and EV had grown up together. In fact, they'd been more like brother and sister until puberty hit and he'd begun to look at her differently. She had deflected him then, and she would deflect him now.

And she would admit to no one, not even Chloe, how his flirting made her feel vital again.

"Yeah? I've seen you in nothing at all."

"We were kids, and you said you wouldn't peek before I had a chance to get into the water."

"I was a hormone infested twelve-year-old and I lied."
Without regret, it seemed.

She scorched him with a look before returning to her seat, her
sandwich, and maybe a little gossip.

At the first bite of soft, yeasty bread filled with sliced turkey,
she closed her eyes and made yummy noises, "Tell David this is a
tiny taste of heaven. I'm glad you two decided to expand the
menu."

"He makes his own aioli." Rhonda paused, a frown marring
her pretty face. "Can I ask you a personal question?"

Too busy eating to answer, EV waved her sandwich to
indicate Rhonda should go ahead.

"Do you really own the whole town and only let in people
who will do whatever you tell them?"

EV nearly choked on a piece of turkey while, behind her, a
guffaw burst from Dalton.

"What the… What?" EV's haste in swallowing the bite of
sandwich had her gulping water to wash it down. She turned to a
red-faced Dalton, "Giggling like that isn't very manly. Get hold of
yourself." He snorted and kept laughing.

"Okay," Rhonda nodded. "I didn't think so, but I had to ask."
Raising her voice, she called out toward the kitchen, "Did you hear
that, David? I told you it was a load of hooey."

"Let me guess, Evan Plunkett."

There was no need for Rhonda to affirm EV's guess, the
answer was written all over her face. "I'm sorry for repeating
such…"

"A load of steaming crap?" EV finished the sentence with a
twinkle in her eye. She had to give it to Rhonda, the younger
woman had guts and, from what she could see, a sense of humor.
"He's only partly right: my family did own the entire town at one
time and, technically, they—we—still own a great deal of land

52

here. If you've read the town charter and history, everything you need to know about my family and their role in Ponderosa Pines is laid out, in black and white."

"I'd just hate for anything to change. We haven't lived here all that long, but we love this place, just the way it is. I don't think we would want to stay if Ponderosa Pines becomes part of Gilmore."

How many others would feel the same?

Chapter 8

Early morning mist hovered over the dew covered grass and was currently soaking through John's running shoes with each stride as he dodged right to cross the churchyard where it bordered his favorite trail. This shortcut was about as close to the Ponderosa Pines Unitarian Universalist Church as he ever went unless forced there by a wedding or a funeral. Some people might need to act pious and sit in pews once a week, but his method of worship was found in that moment when his feet hit the ground and propelled him forward.

Step after step.

Each footfall a prayer.

Running was in his blood to the point where it passed being an obsession and became a compulsion.

Muscles just beginning to loosen and warm up, he noticed out of the corner of his eye that the back door of the church was open. Should he just keep going or check to make sure nothing was wrong? He took three long strides before civic responsibility won out over a hedonistic need for the release of endorphins and he turned back to poke his head in the door.

"Hello?" Dead silence, but for his voice echoed back to him. The last thing he wanted to do was go farther inside; but he did, calling out again all along the hallway that led past a series of empty classrooms and a small kitchenette. Entering the vestibule, he tested the main double doors but they were both locked.

Nothing appeared amiss, but his conscience wouldn't let him just leave without checking the whole building so he stepped through the archway into the chapel proper. The only noise he heard was the whisper of his trainers on the carpet and the gentle whoosh of his own breath.

Eerie stillness crawled across his skin like shivers every time he paused.

Slowly, his feet carried him toward the altar, then behind it to the anteroom which functioned as both storage and the pastor's private office. It was there that he made a grisly discovery.

Luther Plunkett lay dead at the foot of a fallen ladder. John couldn't bring himself to test for a pulse but, he knew from the angle of the contractor's neck and the way his eyes stared fixedly at nothing that it was long past too late.

Swallowing hard kept the contents of his stomach from erupting, but it was a moment or two before he felt capable enough of speech to pull the cell phone out of his pocket and call the authorities. Later, when he told the story, he left out the part where his knees felt shaky at the thought of being alone with a dead body.

It was only a few minutes, but to John it seemed like an age before Doc Talbot walked through the door.

"Nate's on his way. Where's Luther? Show me."

John pointed and Talbot made a beeline to where the contractor lay. "It might be a layman's opinion, but there's not going to be anything you can do to help him." Another shudder ran through him when John recalled the way Luther's eyes had already begun to cloud over.

"No, he's been gone awhile. I need to call it in." Talbot pulled out his cell and spoke quietly into it. "Nate, I'm on the scene. It's

Luther Plunkett. Unattended death." A pause. "Eight hours, give or take."

It was a long time to lay alone, John thought. *Sad how no one had missed the man in all that time.* "Looks like you've got this under control; I'll be going now." John shuffled from one foot to the other. No way he would be finishing his run today. He only hoped the heebie jeebies washed off in the shower because that's where he was headed just as soon as he got out of here.

"You might as well stay; Nate will want to talk to you."

"I'll wait outside then." The air in the church seemed heavy, and when John had cleared the doors, he gulped in deep breaths of clean, pine-scented freshness to clear his head.

* * *

Nate Harper arrived on the scene a few moments later. It seemed like an eternity to poor John, who just wanted to get on with his run where he could find his calm again after such a traumatic experience. Dalton Burnsoll followed behind, looking like a fat kid in a candy store. Wide eyes and an avid expression gave away the fact that he was not a seasoned deputy, and that he was finding his first foray into crime scene investigation positively thrilling.

Regardless of its humble first impressions, the town of Ponderosa Pines hosted rather a lot of expensive, cutting edge green technology. To that end, the board preferred to maintain a small police presence in the form of having at least one resident Deputy. Bud Plaistow filled the law enforcement need for fifteen years, but his recent retirement left a vacancy. For two months the position remained empty until Dalton Burnsoll's surprising renaissance had pushed him into applying for the job.

It had been a stroke of luck when Nate Harper arrived to help train Dalton, even on a temporary basis. Convenient besides, since

Nate had been a darned good homicide cop before his unfortunate injury. His arrival coincided perfectly with Luther's untimely death.

Little did the town know how vehemently Nate did not want to return, and how anxious he was to get back to what he considered his real job. He hoped his shoulder would heal quickly; the less time he had to spend here, the better. The only silver lining he could find was an opportunity to reconnect with Chloe, for whom he had always harbored a crazy, secret crush.

The span of Nate's memory, from childhood to the present, was punctuated by flashes of Chloe. Chloe as a small child, blond pigtails bouncing as she ran ahead of him through a corn field, laughter bubbling from her throat. Chloe as a skinny, pre-teen tomboy, lounging on the stream bank next to him while he reeled in sunfish after sunfish. Chloe as a young girl, beautiful and kind, pulling him into another adventure. Each visit she was a new enigma, transformed by the outside world.

It had never made any sense to pursue her; he knew she wouldn't be staying long and didn't want to ruin their friendship. When she returned to Ponderosa Pines Nate had thought about asking her out on a date. They were closer in actual distance than they had ever been, but part of him wondered how long she'd really stick around. Now, three years later, it didn't look like she was going anywhere, so maybe it was time to find out if she had any romantic interest in him.

Not that he had as much free time as he had expected. It was up to him to train a new deputy, and it was taking more of his time and energy than he originally thought it would.

Eager to please, Dalton resembled a happy puppy, never letting Nate out of his sight for more than a moment and lighting up like a Christmas tree whenever he was given the smallest amount of praise.

For all that, he was actually starting to grow on Nate, who was pleased that someone so zealous had taken up the post. The Pines certainly didn't need the kind of protection Nate was used to offering; he just hoped Dalton would be able to step up to the plate when the time came for Nate to return to his post in the city.

Flashing through town with his lights on turned Nate into the cop equivalent of the Pied Piper. Those who saw him fly by followed and spread the word to everyone else. Within minutes half the town knew something was happening at the church, and quite a few of them gathered outside to gawk and speculate.

Nate took a quick statement from John, who was by this point visibly worn and reaching the end of his rope, and told him it was okay to leave. One look at the crowd out front turned John's feet toward the back door of the church. Nothing mattered more right now than slipping away without fielding the inevitable questions.

"You go; I'll distract them," Nate offered before turning to the crowd milling about the church entrance and making a brief statement while John slid unnoticed into the trees. He made a mental note to thank Nate later before letting the peace of his personal sanctuary provide the balm to soothe his soul.

"There has been an accident here; and, until we have notified the family of the individual involved, I have to ask that you all clear out. We will release a statement as soon as possible. But for now, please let us do what we need to do." Disappointment colored the faces of a few of the nosier residents, but most seemed to understand and the group dissipated.

When Nate finally entered the church to survey the crime scene, Dalton followed. What he saw wiped the elation from his face immediately. Though it was not the first dead body he had ever seen, it was the first time he had been privy to the sight of a person who had met their end in a painful and unnatural way.

Dalton had never cared for Luther Plunkett; they had been thrown together on various town committees over the years, and Luther had always come across as somewhat of an asshat. Still, on a base level, Luther was a human being; and Dalton wasn't one to assume that what someone showed on the outside was necessarily indicative of what was going on inside.

Nate watched as Dalton struggled with the scene before him, watched the emotions play across his new deputy's face: shock, sadness, and anger at the waste of a life all flitted past before he settled on acceptance and determination. It was the exact same experience Nate remembered from his first homicide investigation, and he had seen many a newbie cop who couldn't handle the realities placed before him. Yes, it appeared that Dalton would be more than capable of serving and protecting once he had been fully trained.

Chapter 9

For EV, the perfect day started when she rolled out of bed without having to be awakened by an electronic rooster, padded downstairs in her energy efficient home for a healthy breakfast followed by some time spent tending her gardens. After a steaming hot shower she might boot up her computer to take care of correspondence and whatever tweaks were needed on her family's corporate website before heading out to one of her haunts where she could hear the latest local gossip.

Any grapevine as strong as the one in this small town needed tending, and EV considered herself a gossip gardener. It was her duty to nip off tendrils of exaggeration or prune vines that threatened to produce sour grapes. Half the charm of a small town lay in the willingness of residents to be generally helpful to one another, and she knew the old saying about sticks and stones was a load of crap: words hurt when they were sharpened into barbs by wagging tongues, then slung without thought, but a word or two in the right ear at the right time was often enough to keep neighbors civil.

It was her civic duty to stand guard over the grapevine and not merely her favorite form of entertainment.

Okay, that might be a bit of a stretch.

Today she would be spending the afternoon packing boxes of vegetables at the community food co-op. Arriving early, she stationed herself in the prime spot for overhearing the most conversation. With her back to everyone, filling gallon-sized bags with handfuls of fresh, fragrant green beans, she listened to Mr. Zellner explain his version of events from the night before.

"That Luther doesn't have brains enough to shut up when he's behind. There's obvious benefits to joining up with Gilmore, if he would have explained it right."

Just as she was tempted to turn around and blast his socks off, Horis cut in and did it for her.

"What benefits? Higher taxes? We already have our own school system, our own small police department, and a fair method of government that takes into account the needs and desires of the community. What more do you want?"

Zellner mumbled, "Backwards, back-woods hick."

EV spun around and took a deep breath to let him have it but Horis shook his head. "Save it."

She tried to let it go, but couldn't resist a parting shot. "It's a town, not a cage. You don't need an invitation to move out; you can do that any time."

"Could move to Gilmore without doing a thing, if you'd just play ball." Zellner had to have the last word.

Having made his point, the older man stormed off as fast as his spindly legs would carry him—somewhere around the same pace as a turtle on a cold day—while EV and Horis watched.

Once he was out of earshot, EV turned to Horis, "Is that what everyone wants? For me to shut up and let Gilmore annex us?" An echoing cavern swallowed her stomach. "I never thought…I assumed the town was happy the way we are. Was I wrong?"

Horis shoved at his glasses, the gesture absent-minded as though one he performed many times a day. He laid a hand on her shoulder with a tentative awkwardness that was meant to be

62

comforting. "Zellner thinks chemical pesticides will do a better job of getting rid of the grubs that got into his strawberry patch. Trouble is, he waited so long to do anything about them, they're going to be tough to cull. He's getting too old to push the tiller, and he's too stubborn to ask for help. He figures the more lenient Gilmore regs would let him use chemicals that are easy enough for him to apply himself."

These were the little types of fires EV helped put out on a daily basis. Thanking Horis for the insight, she approached his nearest neighbor and, after a short conversation, hunted down Mr. Zellner.

"I was just talking to Tank, and he said he's been having some trouble with grubs at his place. He's afraid they've been crossing over from his acreage to yours. By way of an apology, he'd appreciate it if you'd let him treat your strawberry patch with a new recipe he wants to try—neem oil mixed with water; sprays on and gets rid of most pests in a few days."

To save face, Zellner blustered a bit before eventually agreeing. Yet, his posture when he walked away seemed stronger, his step lighter, and EV knew she had gained another supporter.

Breathless and pink in the face, Priscilla didn't even bother to drop the kickstand on her bike when she pulled up in front of the co-op to shout, "Luther Plunkett is dead."

* * *

As Chloe approached the neighborhood farmer's market she could tell that something wasn't right. The flurry of activity wasn't light and cheerful as usual; people were up in arms about something.

Maybe Tweedle Dee and Tweedle Dumb are at it again, she thought to herself. Chloe's intention had been to admire the various fruits and vegetables gathered each week from the patches of community gardens speckled across Ponderosa Pines before filling her shopping basket with enough greens and herbs to make a lovely salad for dinner.

Obviously, that wasn't going to happen.

Feeling a hand on her shoulder, Chloe turned and greeted EV with a resounding "What the hell is going on?"

"You haven't heard yet? Our favorite douchebag bit the dust last night, and word on the street says it looks like someone whacked him."

"Have you been watching *The Sopranos* again, EV?" Chloe chortled. "Word on the street."

"Shouldn't you be the one who knows what's happening in this town?" EV shot back with a grin that quickly fell from her face in light of the bad news. Luther might be the worst handyman in the history of home repair, but in his own way, he meant well. You only had to watch him with his wife Talia to know that he loved and respected her, so he must have possessed some redeeming qualities.

With suitably concerned expressions, EV and Chloe linked arms and headed toward the group of citizens gathered in the center of the market.

"This is supposed to be a safe place to live, not a place where people get murdered in a church," someone in the middle of the group shouted.

"We were all at the town meeting the other night, and we all heard several people disagree with Luther's plan for this town. If this deal is going to cause people to get killed, maybe there's more to it than we thought," someone else replied.

"Or maybe he was right, and we need to think about combining with Gilmore so we can have a bigger police force," a third citizen said. That voice Chloe recognized right away. Summer Beckett's nasal tones were as distinctive as her laugh, which sounded like the braying of a donkey.

"Great," EV muttered to Chloe. "Now we get to deal with the fallout from this mess. Luther is screwing us over from beyond the grave." She just knew this was going to light an even bigger fire under Evan's butt and wasn't looking forward to dealing with it. Her words may have sounded callous, but they covered sadness at the loss of one of their own.

Chloe stayed rooted to the spot, listening to the ongoing conversation long after EV headed home. When she felt as though she had gleaned enough information for next week's column, she turned and carried her pitifully empty string bag back the way she came.

On two things everyone agreed: Luther had been found at the bottom of a twelve-foot stepladder, and his neck had snapped on impact. Officially, it was too soon to tell; but rumor had it he had been pushed.

Since too many people might have it out for him, Chloe struggled with finding a clear motive for his murder. Of course, it could have something to do with the annexation proposal, but the details of all that were still too nebulous for anyone to have reacted with this much anger.

It also seemed unlikely that anyone in town would kill over a matter of an overpriced renovation project. Why risk murder when you could simply sue the bastard?

No, it has to be personal, she pondered as she absentmindedly wandered back toward her house. *That's the only logical explanation.*

Since she hadn't picked up any groceries at the market, Chloe decided to whip up something for lunch with what she already had in her cupboards. She was a fairly accomplished cook and kept a well-stocked pantry for situations such as this.

Chloe reached into her refrigerator and assessed her options. Pulling out a bunch of fresh carrots, a red pepper that was nearing the end of the crisp stage, and the last few celery stalks left in the drawer, she began assembling a crudite platter. Equal parts sour cream and leftover homemade mayonnaise went into a bowl with some chopped dill and parsley, and Chloe finished off the dip with a squeeze of a lemon she found buried deep in the produce drawer.

All of the scraps, from the lemon rind to the carrot peels, Chloe packed in a plastic bag and stowed in the freezer. She wasn't one for wasting food, even food that looked inedible to most people. At some point, the delicious tidbits would make their way into stock for a soup.

She quickly skewered cubes of chicken breast and fresh pineapple while a grill pan was heating on the stove top, then popped half a baguette into the oven to warm. Realizing she had too much food, Chloe picked up the phone and invited EV to join her. By the time EV arrived, the kebabs were caramelizing nicely.

"Hey Gossip Girl, what's the skinny?" EV accepted a proffered glass of wine and slid onto a barstool to watch Chloe cook.

"Your pop culture references are a bit outdated," Chloe chided.

"Everything about me is outdated," EV admitted. "I suppose Luther has already become a sainted figure. I know you're not supposed to speak ill of the dead, but how that translates into extolling non-existent virtues is beyond me. He fell off a ladder. It's not like he jumped in front of a bus to save a puppy."

"Rumor has it that it may have been more than a simple slip and fall." Should she tell EV that her altercation with Luther during the meeting was getting a fair amount of play among the gossip mongers? Or did she already know?

Chloe's social media grapevine worked at about the same speed as EV's old-fashioned one, much to their amusement. In fact, Chloe had proposed an experiment where each of them would start a rumor and then see which one spread the quickest.

"And since we argued in a public place, I'm the most likely candidate for being the one to give him a shove." EV waggled her eyebrows in her best menacing manner.

"Yep, that is the current speculation—at least among a small subset of residents. Newcomers mostly. The oldtimers are pretty much split between thinking Luther had an unfortunate accident or was too stupid to be up on that ladder in the first place. On one thing both those factions agree: that was a Nader ladder."

"Unsafe at any speed?"

"Exactly. He's well known for not taking care of his tools."

"Seems funny that his wife didn't miss him. You'd think she would notice he never came home."

Chloe flipped the burner off under the kebabs while saying over her shoulder, "Maybe the rhythm finally got her and she was out shaking it at The Yard again. I don't know. But here's a snippet of next week's column for you: What pair of ornery sisters have been causing embarrassing scenes from The Mudbucket all the way to the chicken coop?"

"Lottie and Talia? What's the beef with them this time?"

"Such is the question on everyone's lips."

"You get all this off the 'net?" As comfortable here as in her own home, EV moved into the kitchen to pull two place settings from Chloe's ruthlessly organized cabinets while the younger woman put the finishing touches on their meal. This kind of thing happened so often the pair of them moved through the compact space with the precision of a water ballet.

"Not this time. Totally old-school. I hit the farmer's market intending to stock up on some fruits and veggies, and instead I got an earful."

Chapter 10

From where Chloe sat at her desk, which fit cozily into the large dormer window on the small second floor of her house, the view inspired her. Red and orange blazed across the sky as the sun set above the section of pond just visible in the distance, and the scent of Heliotropes wafted through the window to caress her face.

The room was originally her mother's master suite, but Chloe preferred it as an office and chose, instead, to reside in one of the smaller bedrooms downstairs. She spent much more time working than she did in her bedroom, and making changes offered her the opportunity to turn the house into her own home. She chewed on the end of a pen and gazed out the window while attempting to come up with a hook for her next column. Keeping things fresh was a big challenge in a small town; one Chloe handled with her usual gusto.

The problem was, very little gossip was new gossip. *Pine Cone* readers were encouraged to utilize an automated telephone tip line if they had any dirt of the juicy variety. Though the tips occasionally netted a viable lead, more often than not they merely sent Chloe searching for geese that had already flown south for the winter. In truth, the line provided more entertainment than anything else.

So, in order to keep her column relevant and authoritative, Chloe relied heavily on social media and direct observation using her highly-honed investigative reporting skills. Community gatherings were always entertaining and informative, allowing her the opportunity to watch from afar without looking suspicious. In fact, she managed to blend so effectively that people often didn't realize she was around, even though she had attended nearly every social function that had taken place in the last three years.

In the interest of keeping her identity as gossip columnist a secret, Chloe steered clear of the *Pine Cone's* official "office", which was a re-purposed storage pod situated in the editor's back yard. The weekly newsletter was a passion project for Wesley, and was compiled by a rotating staff of volunteers in true Ponderosa Pines fashion.

As one might guess, her position was close to unpaid; though, as the only staff member with a recurring column. she was offered a minuscule salary. Combined with the small trust fund left to her by Lila's parents and the fact that her bills were minimal (she owned her home, used solar and wind power, and got most of her food from communal gardens she helped tend) the salary was enough to keep her comfortable.

Much of what made it into her column originated from the web, as people were more than willing to talk about themselves *ad nauseam* on Facebook, Twitter, and the myriad of other social networks that ruled the Internet. The tricky part was sifting through the bull for another angle. It didn't pay to simply repeat what was readily available information in the first place.

No, Chloe used what she learned as a jumping off point, then meticulously checked out each lead online and in person. While people were often a bit too honest about their escapades, they also slanted the truth in their own favor. Cross-referencing allowed her to see both sides of the story and find the truth that usually lay somewhere in between.

Chloe opened Facebook and combed the latest status updates for a few nuggets of useful information. She immediately dismissed the umpteen photographs of people's dinner plates. One neighbor from down the street had made a delicious-looking seafood chowder, but another's husband wasn't going to be happy with a casserole that looked as though it had already been eaten once. *For the love of puppies, nobody cares!*

Instead she clicked on Luther's profile, which had turned into an outlet for grief after his untimely demise.

It was clear that most of what was posted on the late Luther's wall was perfunctory at best, which made Chloe once again feel sorry for the man. At least a little bit. *You reap what you sow.* Equivalent to the standard "Have a great summer" scrawled in the back of every high school yearbook ever made, each successive comment painted a picture of a man with very few close friends and even fewer admirers.

Aside from his wife and brother, Luther had little family left. Neither of them had commented on his wall, which made sense to Chloe. She doubted the first thing she would be doing after losing a loved one was perusing Facebook.

Her only choice was to dedicate this week's column to Luther; it would be tacky and disrespectful to comment on the mundane when the community had lost a member in such a sudden, devastating way. She closed her eyes and conjured as many personal memories of the man as she could, then began to write as heartfelt a eulogy as she could muster.

"...devoted husband to Natalia Plunkett...supporter of the Ponderosa Pines Unitarian Universalist Church...will be missed by many." She knew it was trite but was at a loss, unable to produce more than a base level of sympathy for a man who had contributed so little to her beloved community.

This edition would be clean of the snark she typically relied on, and when she finally hit "print" Chloe let out a sigh of relief that the daunting task was over. She would nonchalantly drop the copy by Wesley's pod later; she always made sure to hand it to him directly. Neither communicated via email to diminish the likelihood that her identity would be revealed.

Foreseeing a need for details, Chloe switched into research mode and began compiling a list of everyone's whereabouts at the time of the murder. Community census results were tabulated frequently and considered public record, so she kept an updated file on her computer at all times.

She printed several copies, tucked a few away in her field notebook, and started marking one up with notes. When her personal observances had been notated, she reopened several web browsers and began to search for status updates and location tags for the time frame surrounding the town meeting.

Irritation aimed at herself colored Chloe's face as she realized she had forgotten to call the tip line. Each week, her routine started out the same. She would listen to the voice mails left on the *Pine Cone*'s tip line and forward any legitimate news to Wesley, then check the newsletter's email, Facebook and Twitter accounts.

Blaming preoccupation for causing her to skip her usual first step, she now pressed the speaker button on her desk phone and hit the number two key to speed-dial the tip line mailbox.

"You have no new messages," the electronic voice rang out.

That's a little odd. You'd think every amateur sleuth in town would be calling to lend a theory about old Luther's unfortunate slip. Assuming the system was down again Chloe vowed to call the answering service first thing in the morning and submit a help-desk ticket.

Beep boop beep. Nate's profile picture popped up on the edge of Chloe's computer screen.

"Burning the midnight oil again?" read his text message. Chloe looked up and realized the sky was now black and that she hadn't eaten a thing since the veggie burrito she scarfed around noon.

"Midnight? It's only 9:30, Grandpa. Feel like grabbing a bite to eat? I know the 65-and-older menu at Mama Nancy's only runs 'til 8:00, but I'll chip in the extra 10 percent."

"I'm choosing to ignore that remark, though I won't forget it. And I will eat you under the table. Be ready in 10 minutes."

* * *

Chloe snapped her computer lid shut and ran downstairs to find a sweater. A quick glance in the mirror showed that all she needed was to tame a few flyaway hairs around her face and apply a fresh coat of mascara. By the time she was finished, Nate was knocking on the door and leading her out to his car, a black 1967 Chevrolet *Camaro* with chrome rims he had affectionately dubbed *Shannon* after the song he heard on the radio the first time he drove it.

The car was a near replica of the one from *Better Off Dead*, her favorite '80's movie, and she loved to drive it. Nate knowingly held the ignition key in an outstretched hand as Chloe sailed past him and into the driver's seat. Stealing a glance at his posture, she was happy to see that at least one person in town wasn't scared to death by her driving style.

By the time Chloe whipped into a parking space at Mama Nancy's Diner, her blood was pumping from the exhilaration of having thousands of pounds of responsive machinery completely under her command. The car cornered like it was on rails. Nate walked around to meet her, hand held out for his keys; but, with a saucy grin, she pocketed them for the ride home.

Inside the diner, a sign directed them to choose an empty seat so Nate led the way to one of the cozier corner booths where he ordered the heart-attack special; a platter piled high with deep fried appetizers. Chloe bit into a fat onion ring and closed her eyes for a moment to savor the crispy goodness before nudging Nate's foot under the table and tilting her head toward the rest of the patrons. The gleam in her eye told him she was ready for a round of their favorite game of people watching. The diner was dimly lit at night, a cone of golden light illuminating the center of each table and lending an air of mystery to the surrounding patrons. Chloe took a sip of her drink, gestured toward a booth across the room and challenged "Game on, corner booth."

Nate surveyed the couple for a moment before commenting "Blind date. Has to be. She's dressed to impress, sitting in a diner with a man who looks like an insurance salesman. Her knees are together, pointed away from him while his body language is urgent and definitely interested. He was hoping to score, but I don't see that happening. See, she just checked the clock and is now searching for the bathroom."

"Good call; I believe you're right. I just hope it wasn't a good friend who set her up, because she's never going to forgive for this one. How much you wanna bet she climbs out the window?"

"You're on. Now you, table by the door. What's the story with this group?"

"Church group or Amway meeting, could go either way. Definitely stopping over from some kind of convention. I bet their little minibus is full of briefcases and inspirational pamphlets."

Nate laughed out loud and turned his attention to another couple. As he debated over their situation, Chloe watched him chew thoughtfully on a piece of deep-fried pickle. His strong jaw was covered with a couple of day's worth of stubble, and Chloe imagined that he had decided he didn't need a clean shave to watch over the hippies at Ponderosa Pines. The scruff made him look a bit older than usual; and, for the first time Chloe could see him as something other than the childhood pal he had always been to her.

Nate raked a hand through his tawny hair, making it stand up in all directions. It was a gesture she remembered well, having seen him do it more times than she could count. As she reached up automatically to smooth it back into place, he flashed a dimpled smile that would turn most women to butter.

When he excused himself to go to the restroom, she noticed the way his hips moved and had to look away as her cheeks turned a rosy shade of pink. He didn't seem to notice, so she assumed they

74

had returned to their normal color by the time he returned to the table.

"So are we going to talk about the elephant in the room, or what?" It was Nate who asked the question, even as Chloe was silently wondering the same thing. "What do you and your sidekick know about Luther that I don't know?" He asked, quirking an eyebrow to suggest that it didn't please him one bit to be fishing for information. His pride was taking a hit; and, as a man who was usually top dog, it felt a bit too much like failure for his liking.

It was no secret that Nate didn't feel exactly the same way as Chloe did about Ponderosa Pines. Of course he loved his childhood home, felt a feeling of camaraderie with many of his former neighbors, and agreed that he wouldn't be happy if the town were to become less than what it always had been. But that didn't mean he particularly wanted to live there full time. Not all his memories were warm and fuzzy, and he didn't need a daily reminder.

Chloe nibbled a mozzarella stick for a moment before answering, "Luther was a liar and a cheat when it came to his work. His brother controlled him, used him as a puppet to get ahead as long as it suited him. He's been the voice of Evan's campaign to merge with Gilmore, but you could tell it wasn't his idea; he wasn't smart enough for that. I don't know why someone would kill him for that, though, or even over a shoddy construction job. It seems personal. Maybe he pissed his brother off; I don't know. But I do know that people are speculating that EV had something to do with it, and that's just preposterous."

"Because he was on opposing sides? There's nothing EV Torrence likes more than a good argument, and if you know that Evan was pulling the strings then she knows it too. There's no real motive for EV to have killed him. But it still doesn't look good that she got into a public argument with him right before he died. I'll have to check out all viable leads, so don't be surprised when she gets questioned." Nate's tone was authoritative, and Chloe sensed he was shifting into cranky cop mode.

The sight of EV being hauled out of the Pines in a squad car wouldn't help her and Chloe's plan to convince the townspeople to remain separate from Gilmore. Hopefully Nate would be able to investigate quietly. A scandal would not help EV's position. Nate was right; she and EV always did have an in on the goings on about town, and maybe it was about time to put that little talent to good use. If they could help him solve this murder that much faster, maybe EV could stay out of the limelight.

"Hey, tell me a story about these three hot messes walking in right now." Chloe changed the subject, deciding not to show any more of her cards until she could talk to EV and formulate a plan.

* * *

Chloe generously tipped the waitress as Nate handled the dinner bill. Years ago Chloe had bet Nate a lifetime of free dinners that she could beat him at darts. He had pompously accepted the wager before realizing he had been hustled. Having waited tables for room and board money during college she understood how much each party's gratuity contributed to a waitress's nightly total, so when service was excellent she made sure to tip accordingly.

Waitress was just one of the job titles Chloe had held throughout the years. After completing high school via correspondence course while traveling with her mother, Chloe put her foot down and attended a brick and mortar college like a normal person.

Six years, and almost as many majors later, she graduated with honors and a degree in journalism. Still feeling unfulfilled, Chloe worked her way through a succession of different jobs looking for something that felt like the right fit. For now, with the restlessness tamed, she was committed to maintaining her post as author of 'Babble & Spin' while submitting the occasional freelance article for extra cash. If the restlessness returned, she' deal with it somehow.

76

With a gentlemanly hand on Chloe's back, Nate guided her toward the restaurant's exit door. Stopping to grab the light sweater she had hung in the entryway, Chloe heard a loud crash and turned in the direction of the kitchen. Huddled in a booth around the corner from where she and Nate had dined sat Evan Plunkett. And he wasn't alone. Seated across from him was a woman of average build, her hair bound in an updo and covered by a familiar floral print scarf.

Chloe gestured to Nate. "Do you recognize that woman in the scarf? I saw Talia Plunckett wearing that exact same one the other night at The Barnyard!

"It's just a scarf; anyone could have one like it. I can't tell who it is for certain from this angle."

"Nate, it's a vintage Pucci." Chloe stated with a roll of her eyes.

"It's a what-ti? What does that even mean?" his face held the expression typical of men who knew they had treaded into murky waters.

"He was a famous scarf desig—you know what, never mind. Just trust me when I say that only one person in the vicinity has that scarf. That also doesn't look like someone comforting his dead brother's wife; it looks intimate."

Nate shot one last look in the direction of Evan and the mystery woman's table and pulled Chloe out the door. "Let's not get caught staring. I don't need him thinking I'm following him, especially if there is something nefarious happening here."

Chapter 11

"Talia and Evan?" EV mused when Chloe finished bringing her up to speed on what she had seen the night before. "I don't see it." She shook her head, "Between you and me, I always thought Talia only tolerated Evan for Luther's sake."

"I know, but I know what I saw, or at least what I think I saw. Seriously, what are the chances that there are two vintage Pucci scarves of the same design in Ponderosa Pines?"

"Somewhere between slim and none," EV shook her head again. Evan and Talia? She shuddered at the thought. "It had to be her."

"You think she killed Luther? Or was it a Cain and Abel thing and Evan did the deed?"

Shrugging, EV said, "What did Nate say? He was there, he must have added them to the list of suspects."

"I don't know. He dragged me out of there and refused to talk about it again. There's gossip about Evan seeing a married woman. Talia is definitely a married woman, so it fits. And hey...the scarf. What else could it be?" Chloe's tone and the hand she waved in the air expressed the opinion her theory was correct.

"You're sure they weren't just talking family business?" Chloe rolled her eyes. "Okay, but I still find it hard to picture mousy little Talia shoving poor dumb Luther off a ladder."

"What about Evan? You know him better than I do."

"That's the thing; I'm not sure I do. I would never have expected him to have an affair with Talia. Not because she is his brother's wife, but because she's Talia. Not his type of woman at all: too much of a homebody. Evan likes them a little less…tamed."

Pent up energy pulled Chloe to her feet and had her pacing. "I wish we could get a look at the…" she swallowed hard, "where it happened. Nate could have missed something, and now that we know who the UNSUB might be…"

"You've been watching too many episodes of *Criminal Minds*." EV shrugged off the heat from Chloe's glare.

"*Matlock*."

"Puhlease. Andy Griffith never uttered that word and you know it. Matlock, really? I'm old and I don't even watch that one."

Chloe sniffed and ignored the dig, "I'm merely suggesting we do our civic duty," she responded primly.

"You really are a *Matlock* fan."

"You are twisted and evil." There was no malice, though, behind the words, and Chloe had to grin when EV loosed her best evil laugh.

During the hour the two had spent discussing recent events the summer sky had begun to fill with ominous looking clouds. EV's weather sense predicted a short burst of rain followed by clearing skies and raised humidity as the sun beat wet earth into steamy submission.

"Walk, ride, or drive?" EV hoped Chloe wouldn't offer to drive. Her little car was a menace and only half because of its driver. Just four years old, not a single fender had escaped some form of injury.

"My legs could use the stretch; let's walk."

The Wiggle Leg trail was the most direct route since it cut straight through the woods to bypass a mile-long twisted section of road that took only marginally less time to drive than to walk.

EV handed Chloe a spare umbrella and a bottle of water before striding off at a pace the younger woman had to push a little to maintain. Not surprising since Chloe's legs were almost a foot shorter.

Chloe refused to be outdone, so she picked up the pace.

EV lengthened her stride.

Chloe walked faster.

By the time they reached the center of town, both women were glowing from the effort.

"Was that a walk or a forced march?" Chloe bent double to stretch out tingling muscles.

"Just think, you won't have to get on that hamster wheel you call a treadmill and trudge along to nowhere later," EV smirked.

"Bite me."

The sight of the church spire in the distance sobered the pair of them. A man had died there. True, he was not one of their favorite people, but neither of them had wished for his death.

"How are we going to get in?" Chloe asked. It might have sounded like a good idea at the time, but breaking into a church would probably ensure she went straight to hell. "You think one of the windows will be open?"

"Maybe. Or we could just use this key," EV pulled a small brass key from her pocket.

"Fine, do it the easy way."

Even from where they stood at the end of the street, the bright yellow crime scene tape stood out in stark relief against the weathered, gray wood exterior of the church. A wall of heavy blue storm clouds hunkered behind the white spire like something evil waiting to pounce.

Chloe shivered.

Focused straight ahead, EV strode toward the church, and making no effort at concealing herself or her intent, twisted the key in the lock then ducked under the yellow tape to push the door open.

Evidence tampering.

That's what she would be charged with; Chloe wasn't looking forward to going to jail.

She followed EV who seemed to know exactly where she was going.

In the end, there was nothing much to see. Scattered tools and an overturned ladder were the only items marking the spot where Luther had died.

"Epic anti-climax," Chloe pointed out.

"You think so?" EV waved a hand toward where the ladder lay folded. "I've learned at least two things already."

"What?" Maybe it was trepidation keeping her normally keen mind obscured, but Chloe saw nothing suggestive in the scene that lay before her.

"We've been assuming the murderer pushed Luther off the ladder; but, if that had been the case, the ladder would still be standing. Plus, it would have had to be facing this direction," she indicated the only space wide enough to have held the ladder with both legs spread "So it had to have been pushed over sideways. I know from personal experience how rickety this ladder can be; it was my turn to change the light bulbs last month, and Luther loaned it to the church." A touch of sorrow crept into her voice, "He was always good about that kind of thing." It was the first time since the news of his death that she had really taken the time to think about their community losing one of their own. Hapless and short-sighted though he was, Luther, at the bottom of it all, was not such a bad guy.

"And there's no way it was an accident?"

From behind her, Nate answered Chloe's question, "That's what we professionals are paid to determine."

"Busted."

"Totally," Nate agreed. "Breaking and entering, tampering with evidence, public nuisance," he ticked offenses off wryly.

"I have a key, so I don't think you can make the B&E stick. I'm pretty sure you can't get us for public nuisance," Ev held out her wrists, "we haven't touched a thing. But go ahead and arrest me, Nathaniel. It wouldn't be my first time."

Making a note to grill EV for details at her earliest convenience, Chloe stepped forward to lay a hand on Nate's forearm. She ignored the tingle of warmth that traveled through her fingertips where they lay over strong muscles. "There's no reason to do anything hasty."

Dalton walked through the door, hands streaming with the yellow tape he had been instructed to pull down from outside. Catching sight of the tableau before him, he carelessly tossed the tape down on the last pew and hurried toward where Nate and EV faced off.

"Let's everybody calm down, now." Any chance of his getting a date with EV would fly out the window if Nate clapped the cuffs on her. "We were coming here to take down the tape so Pastor could open up for Sunday anyway. Cut them some slack."

"A good lawyer would get the charges dropped anyway." Chloe hoped this was true.

Nate grinned and the tension fell away. "I was just trying to give her a scare. Besides, I know EV wouldn't have called just any lawyer; she'd have done something much worse. She would have called…"

"…his mother," EV finished for him.

Chapter 12

Chloe threw a bundle of dried sage into the center of the fire pit, leaned in and inhaled deeply as the scented smoke curled around her face. One by one she lit the torches encircling the small patio situated in a secluded corner of her backyard. An ancient fence covered in clematis and honeysuckle bordered the area on two sides. Pathways led to the house in one direction and through a break in the fence toward EV's backyard in another. Since Chloe moved back to town, that path had widened and become worn with use as it had been when her mother lived here.

Chloe's roots in Ponderosa Pines ran almost as deep as EV's. Her grandparents were among the founding members of the community. Chloe's mother and EV, born within days of each other, had grown up practically as sisters. However, the two could not have differed more in their opinion of their childhood home. EV had no desire to leave while Lila's wanderlust, combined with a heavy helping of ambition, drove her to the ends of the earth dragging Chloe along for the ride.

Lila, upon learning of Chloe's decision to return to the Pines, applied every tool in her arsenal with the intention of changing her daughter's mind. When those efforts met with no success, she fired a final, parting shot by letting Chloe know, in no uncertain terms, that Lila herself would not be returning. Ever.

With the implied ultimatum hanging over her head and resolve stiffening her spine, Chloe had loaded up the meager possessions accumulated after years of moving from one place to the next and driven away. The tears that ran down her face spoke of both sadness and joy as she began the journey toward the one place she remembered being completely happy, Ponderosa Pines.

Arriving in the middle of the night, Chloe felt the rightness of her decision the minute the key slid home in the lock. She twisted the key, then the knob. When the door swung open, her feet carried her without hesitation to switch on what she remembered as the ugliest lamp in existence. She felt the contentment of being home slide over her like a soft blanket.

If that minute hadn't been enough to convince her she had made the right decision, forming a firm bond with her next door neighbor and her mother's oldest friend, EV, cemented the deal.

"Speak of the devil," Chloe mused with a grin as EV appeared next to her.

"I brought stuff for s'mores!" EV replied.

"Traditional or peanut butter cup?"

"Both, of course." EV rolled her eyes. "Not my first campfire."

Chloe stuck her tongue out at her friend.

"It's not so dark I can't see that. So who do we think dunnit? Evan? Talia? Some shadowy figure from Luther's past? Or just a ticked off customer who didn't like the way he installed their bathroom tile?" EV began.

"Don't be so flip; people think YOU dunnit, and that's nothing to smile about."

"People in this place know it wasn't me. And since I didn't do it, the best we can hope for is to help Nate and Dalton figure who did. Do we agree that it had to be someone who was at the town meeting the other night?"

Taking a moment to ponder, Chloe answered, "I think that's what everyone is thinking, which in itself makes me suspicious. I suppose we should consider motives and then run through the list of likeliest suspects. But, I have to say, it gives me the creeps in a big way to think one of us would do something like that. This is Ponderosa Pines, after all, and ..."

"Nothing bad ever happens in Ponderosa Pines." They sing-songed together.

She pulled out her tablet and sent EV back home for hers before selecting a plump marshmallow and poking it through the center with the end of a stick. They did this so often Chloe had cut and sharpened special s'mores sticks from a stand of alders that bordered the far edge of her yard. These were now tucked into a basket near the edge of the patio.

No stranger to technology, EV kept up to date with her electronic devices. Where she differed from Chloe was that she preferred human contact to the techno variety. She got her gossip straight from the source whenever possible so she could evaluate the body language that went along with it. Yet, she would not argue that people often felt protected by the seeming anonymity of the Internet and let things slip that they never would admit to in person. The result? Between the two of them, they learned just about everything of interest that ever happened in Ponderosa Pines. They heard plenty of things that were not interesting as well, come to that.

EV began noting down names beginning with those who never failed to turn out for every town meeting. Most were long-term residents with a higher stake in how decisions were made—business owners, founding family members—or out and out busybodies who could not bear to have anything happen without them knowing every detail.

Chloe produced the copy of the community census she had begun marking up before her dinner with Nate. "Well, I think we can safely cross your fan club, the Landry's, Horis, and Priscilla off the list, since I can't imagine how any of their lives would change with Luther gone."

"And I heard Celia and Bert going at it half the night that night."

"Fighting?" Chloe smelled gossip.

"No, the other thing." A cheeky grin accompanied EV's waggling eyebrows.

"Oh. Ew."

"Bert has a surprising amount of stamina for a man his age."

Laughing but holding up a hand, Chloe declared, "TMI. Seriously. Just way too much information."

Nodding, EV crossed the two names off the list, but couldn't resist adding, "Celia's a bit of a screamer."

"Why? Why would you tell me that? You have to stop. Really."

"Put that in your column. I dare you." Another eyebrow waggle garnered EV a set of rolling eyes.

"Enough of that. I mean it. No more mental images that I will never be able to unsee."

"Okay, back to our list." An unrepentant EV tapped the stylus on the screen thoughtfully, "Goes without saying Talia and Evan take the top two places."

"You think?"

"Love and money are the main reasons for killing someone; and if Talia and Evan really are doing the wild thing on the side, they'd have the most reason for shoving poor Luther off a ladder."

"Nate says he's sure it wasn't either one of them."

"Then we need to see some evidence. Don't get me wrong, I know the boy means well and he's good at his job, but we have the deeper insights and way better contacts then he does. If anyone is going to solve this, it'll be us."

"True." Chloe handed EV a peanut butter cup s'more, exchanged it for the tablet, and jotted down the names of some of Luther's disgruntled former clients. "Here's what strikes me funny about all this: I can't see Evan and Talia together. Okay, I might have *seen* it, assuming it was Talia in that scarf at the diner, but I don't know; it doesn't make much sense at all. He's just not the settle-down type, and she totally is."

"I thought she and Luther seemed happy. She's always so meek and subdued; I can't see her getting up the gumption to kill her husband. It just feels all kinds of wrong."

"The way they were dancing the other night seemed plenty happy. Maybe a little too happy for a public venue."

Chapter 13

On the day of Luther's funeral, thick fog descended to lay like a pall over Ponderosa Pines: its mass so dense the air struggled to carry its moist weight. From above, the church spire was the only visible landmark as it speared through the heavy vapor that lay close along the ground.

Knuckles white on the steering wheel and a tension headache threatening, Chloe hunched forward in an effort to see two feet beyond the nose of her car while beads of moisture continually formed on her windshield.

From the normally throaty *purr* of the car's engine to the clicking of the wiper blades, every sound was muted as though the blanket of heavy mist had actually been made of the white wool it resembled.

"You think there'll be a big turnout?" Chloe ignored the way EV's foot kept punching the imaginary passenger-side brake. Maybe a little conversation would help break the tension.

"Well, you know funerals are always a big deal here in the Pines; but with Luther being murdered and the church being the crime scene, it will be packed to the rafters."

"Which means the murderer will be in attendance, then."

"I think we can count on it, so keep your eyes and ears open."

"Duh, gossip columnist, remember? My eyes and ears are always open."

"Deer!" EV shouted.

"I see it." Chloe stomped the brake hard. She kept the car at little more than a crawl, but the sudden stop still set her heart racing and the pies lining the back seat skittering very close to the edge. The doe stared at them for a moment before meandering out of harm's way.

What was normally a five-minute walk had taken nearly three times that to drive. Why had they thought bringing four kinds of pie was a good idea?

Since they were arriving almost an hour early for the service and more people would be walking than driving, Chloe easily found a parking spot close to the church. Offering to help with setting up had been her idea, and it was a good one. The more time spent with Talia, the better the chance she might let some useful information slip.

Plus, it was a lead-pipe cinch that her sister, loud-mouth Lottie, would be there and that woman couldn't keep a secret if her life depended on it. Maybe they could learn something new about the ongoing feud between the sisters while appearing sympathetic for Talia's loss.

Two steps from the car, they could already hear her booming voice berating the widow for her choice of casket. "It doesn't go with the flowers. Honestly, Talia, you have the worst taste. If it had to be gray, you could at least have gone with charcoal instead of this ugly silver color."

"I don't recall asking for your opinion, you fat cow; so maybe you should keep it to yourself." Talia's normally meek voice screeched through the window.

Chloe and EV exchanged wide-eyed grins. Apparently becoming a widow had turned Talia from a mouse to a lion.

"Well, I never." Lottie's voice rang out with shock.

Talia snorted. "Well, maybe you should. It would improve your temperament and probably clear up that skin problem."

Chloe clapped a hand over her mouth to keep the giggle from escaping while EV's grin just got wider. Now this was a side of Talia she could grow to like. At the sound of footsteps approaching, both women pasted on their best serious expressions and managed to wipe away the last vestiges of mirth before an angry Lottie burst through the door to enter the vestibule. She scowled at seeing EV standing there, then shot her nose into the air and marched out of the church.

Before they could turn and walk through the door, Chloe and EV heard Talia speaking to Luther where he lay amid the coffin pillows. "I'm sorry you had to hear that, Luther. I know you've always expected me to turn the other cheek, but today I've run out of cheeks." Emotion choked her voice, "Now, you sleep easy and don't worry about me. I can take care of myself."

Waiting until Talia fell silent, EV finally pushed through the doors, and with Chloe following her, stepped into the church proper. The widow stood head down with one hand resting on Luther's where they lay folded; the perfect picture of heartbreak.

Until now, it hadn't occurred to either of them that Talia might be among the small contingent who considered EV a suspect in Luther's death. So when Chloe moved forward to offer a consoling hug, EV remained behind to gauge Talia's reaction.

After gratefully accepting the hug, Talia, eyes brimming, crossed over to where EV still stood and practically launched herself into EV's arms, which answered the question quite nicely.

"What am I going to do now? Luther was my whole life," she wailed.

Genuinely sorry for the woman, EV hugged her hard. "I'm so sorry, Talia. What can we do to help?"

Chloe looked around the room; everything seemed ready. The casket sat amid a pitifully small selection of flower arrangements, which seemed sad considering the number of people who would soon be crowding the pews. The pulpit was stationed near where Luther's head rested and at his feet stood a small table with a video memorial scrolling endlessly through a lifetime of photos.

To the casual observer, the images would be little more than a catalog of a life sadly shortened; but to Chloe, who had more experience in reading body language than most, they showed an innocent child becoming an increasingly unhappy boy before growing into a hardened man. Only in the photos of him with Talia did she see anything soft or loving; in those, he became a different person altogether. One she actually felt sorry for.

Visibly calmer than when they had arrived, Talia answered, "There's really nothing left to do, so if you could just sit with me for a little while…" The slamming open of the door heralded Lottie's re-entry as she stalked back to where her sister sat.

"I'll forgive you that last remark because I know you're distraught," she announced. "Anyone would be under the circumstances."

Before Talia had time to respond, the door opened again and the first of the mourners made their way toward the front of the church. Talia stood to greet them while EV quietly asked Lottie, "Where's Evan? Shouldn't he be here?"

"He's probably outside waiting to make an entrance," contempt dripped from every word. "All he seems to care about is whether or not Luther left a will. He's hardly said a word to Talia otherwise." Her contempt for Luther and his family was well known. She settled her black-clad self upon the pew next to EV and Chloe. "Did she tell you about the notes?" Her voice lowered to a stage whisper. "Someone has been blackmailing Evan."

Chloe and EV's eyes met; finally, some interesting news.

EV chose her words carefully so as not to be seen trying to pry, "How do you know? Have you told the police? They're the best ones to handle something like this."

"I hear things, but I don't always tell everything I know."

That was the last chance for private conversation before a combination of actual mourners and curiosity seekers filled the pews. It was easy to tell the difference. Those who truly felt Luther's loss made their way up front where Talia stood in unrelieved black to give their condolences, while the looky-loos filed into their seats and gossiped in furious whispers about how Luther had died and who might have had motive to kill him. EV garnered more than her fair share of speculative looks.

Evan was one of the last to approach the casket. He moved slowly, shoulders sagging with exaggerated grief in what could only be construed as an attempt to garner sympathy from prospective supporters. EV knew him well enough to know that it wasn't all posturing, but was so disgusted with the act that she couldn't bring herself to feel sorry for him.

He approached Talia and awkwardly wrapped his arms around her with a quick glance back at the crowd. It seemed the most appropriate thing in the world, for a brother to console his widowed sister-in-law, but her reaction showed she felt his gesture out of place and unwelcome. When she didn't respond Evan pulled away, patted her shoulder awkwardly, and then took his seat in the front row.

"That was odd. Why wouldn't she accept his condolences? He's the only other person here who lost as much as she just did."

"Maybe she doesn't want everyone in town to know how close they really are." Chloe replied, waving her eyebrows suggestively.

EV shushed her as the pastor moved toward the podium.

Chapter 14

Nearly two weeks after Luther Plunkett's funeral, everyone, save for his wife and brother, needed to focus on happier matters. Ponderosa Pines' annual Moonlight Madness festival was a big enough ordeal to lift the layer of macabre that had woven its way through town, settling on fence posts and filling every dark corner like thick cobwebs.

The notoriety gained by the Pines for being a green community paled before the town's reputation for hosting a series of outlandish events. Moonlight Madness held the honor of being a favorite among the seasoned residents, as well as the newer arrivals. Festivities began at dusk in the town square before eventually moving to an enormous bonfire in the field beyond the Fairy Garden.

Arms laden with bags of glow sticks and a trail of children following behind her from tallest to shortest like a family of ducklings, Veronica arrived in Chloe's driveway.

"Hello, my darlings," Chloe cooed, kissing each one on the forehead before relieving Veronica of half the shopping bags and depositing them into the trunk of her tiny car. The back seat was completely stuffed with decorations, giving the impression of a clown car ready to burst at any moment.

"Thanks for taking those over. We've got to go back home and get the supplies together for the face painting booth. My arm is going to be Jell-o by the end of the day!"

Veronica's artistic flair and her way with a brush had landed her with the unenviable chore of manning the very popular face-painting booth for three years running. During the first year, delighted at being asked, she had thrown herself into each tiny masterpiece. The second year, her delight lessened considerably when the number of faces to paint doubled and she had barely been able to make it to the bonfire. By the third year, when begging had not released her from the onerous duty, she took the opportunity to add something inappropriate to the faces of anyone who had annoyed her in any way throughout the past year. Always clever, her targets rarely noticed the naughty images in Veronica's handiwork. But for those few in the know, trying to pick out the subtle references added another layer of fun to the madness.

Short minutes later, Chloe pulled into a parking space across from the town square and popped the trunk. Before she could step out of the car she noticed Allegra Worth hobbling across the park toward her car, which was sitting only two spaces away from Chloe's. The tension around her mouth showed as her lips settled into a thinner line each time one of her spiked heels sunk into the grass. Ashton followed closely behind her, Allegra's purse clutched in one hand, looking more like her assistant than her husband.

A giggle threatened to erupt in Chloe's throat, but she stifled it. Each time Allegra yanked her heel out of the turf, her bent leg gave her the look of a demented stork. Chloe sank further in her seat and peeked through the car window. The last thing she wanted to deal with right now was that obnoxious woman.

If she had to guess, Chloe would say Allegra probably topped out at five foot eight; but it was impossible to tell her actual height since she wouldn't be caught dead wearing anything shorter than a three-inch heel. Her age was another mystery, but Chloe would bet money Allegra had recently slid into her forties. She reminded Chloe of a Barbie doll dressed up as Cruella DeVille for Halloween: all of her parts were perfect on their own—shapely legs, a tiny waist, toned arms—but there was something angular and almost odd about the way they all came together. She was certainly attractive, but in a severe, almost cold way.

When the coast was clear, Chloe emerged from the driver's seat and surveyed the park with an unobstructed view. White string lights stretched zig-zagging across the grassy expanse to form a glowing canopy that would, after dark, resemble a twinkling night sky. Star and moon-shaped cutouts would soon hang from tree branches and between the booths that were beginning to pop up in a semi-circle around the park center. The area was abuzz with activity, and Chloe was happy to help.

Lanterns lit a path through a circle of trees and into a clearing where several telescopes were ready and waiting for curious eyes to peer at the cosmos. Another path would lead through the fairy garden and into a field where Chloe knew several citizens were currently constructing the pyre for the bonfire that would commence after dark.

As she moved about hanging pinatas, setting up booths, and making small talk with a few townspeople, Chloe thought back to the first year she had helped with the event. Not having been in town for more than a few weeks, it was still a challenge for her to remember names and relationships, making social interactions a necessary but uncomfortable evil.

Chloe's solution was to do more listening than talking. Now, the secrecy requirements of her work carried on the tradition, and she realized she was slipping into old habits: focus on work; shut out the rest of the world. What was the point of calming down, moving home and settling in if she was going to repeat past mistakes? Vowing to be more friendly and outspoken in the future, Chloe finished up her duties and headed home to get ready for what would surely prove a fun and interesting evening.

* * *

The bonfire was in full swing when Chloe and EV arrived. Nestled into a pair of folding canvas camp chairs atop a gentle rise they sat back and watched the sparks fly high into the air while their friends and neighbors danced to the beat of at least a dozen different hand drums. A positive energy radiated from the crowd, as though they were throwing all cares and woes into the flames and allowing them to dissipate with the billowing pillar of smoke.

Moonlight, combined with the glimmer of firelight, made the dozens of glow sticks bobbing across the field almost unnecessary. Tents of various colors, some makeshift in design, dotted the area surrounding the bonfire. Though living in the Pines often felt akin to camping, this night of the year, especially, people seized the opportunity to sleep beneath the stars. Those who had consumed too many cups of Ponderosa Punch could often be found sprawled on the grass the next morning.

The drumming ceased momentarily, and two voices rose above the din. Lottie and Talia were at it again. Exchanging glances, Chloe and EV circled around the fire, broke off from the group, and made their way toward a clump of trees near where the two were arguing.

"…Don't want to think about it right now, Lottie. Just let me deal with things my own way. For once in your life, BUTT OUT!"

Lottie opened her mouth to retort, but seeing the determined look on Talia's face and the way her hands were shaking in anger she instead turned and stalked away through the trees without another word.

* * *

Having returned to their perch on the hill after another hour of fire dancing, Chloe and EV once again observed the crowd that was still milling around the dwindling bonfire. This time they were accompanied by Mindy and her boyfriend. Jace leaned over to give EV a kiss on the cheek before settling down on the quilt spread out beneath them.

"Don't take this nonsense seriously; we all know if you were going to bump someone off you'd get away totally clean." He teased, bringing a smile to EV's face.

"Remind me to send a pan of mac and cheese to your house, Jace." EV's homemade recipe was well known as the best in town, and she typically only pulled it out for special occasions.

It looked like she may have learned her lesson earlier in the day when, looking much more approachable in sneakers and jeans, Allegra Worth walked past with the ever-faithful Ashton following close behind. Allegra's eyes scanned the crowd as though trying to pick out a single face while Ashton's were trained squarely, as usual, on her.

"Hey, Ashton got the Veronica treatment. Wait, are those man bits on his face?" EV pointed and the rest of the group took a closer look.

"Sure looks like it. He must have gotten on Veronica's list somehow. Maybe he said something snarky. You think he'll ever realize she got the last laugh?"

Chapter 15

From its humble beginnings as a commune, Ponderosa Pines had grown into a fine, if somewhat eclectic, town full of people from varied backgrounds with an interest in living green; but, more importantly, in being part of a tightly knit community.

With a lifetime of history in this place, EV was not interested in seeing the Pines become the type of town governed by one person. The Selectmen system worked well here. Three leaders meant three varying perspectives on every issue. To her, the terms *mayor* and *dictator* were very similar in concept, and the worst-case scenario imaginable would be to have Evan in charge. He already had a Napoleon complex—making him mayor would puff him up beyond all reason. As long as she drew breath, EV vowed to keep that disaster from happening.

If she had to, she could pull rank. As the largest landowner and the only daughter of the founding family, her opinion held enough authority to put a stop to the whole thing. Playing that card, though, was not in her nature; and, in reality, there would likely be little need for her to do so. Despite Evan's assertions, EV would always side with her neighbors in whatever they thought was best for their town. Even if that meant letting Gilmore annex Ponderosa Pines.

Whether Evan realized it or not, almost no one backed him in his bid to become mayor even if Ponderosa Pines combined with Gilmore. For some reason, he had gotten it into his head that EV wanted the job and that her insistence on a more equitable form of town government covered up a plot to keep him from ever holding office.

The man was completely deluded. Running Ponderosa Pines was not on EV's list of fun things to do.

Ever.

Worse still, EV knew he was a main force behind the rumor that she was the one who pushed Luther off the ladder. What kind of lowlife would use his own brother's death to get ahead?

All she wanted was to live a peaceful life in her peaceful town; but no matter what anyone said, she would never kill to make that happen—okay, maybe in fantasy, but never in reality.

Luther had been a liar and a cheat, but neither of those things had him topping her imaginary hit list. Everyone had their secrets—maybe not as many as they liked to think. The grapevine here in the Pines had deep roots and tendrils that snaked everywhere, and EV was tapped in more than most.

She knew Luther padded his estimates—hell, everyone knew that. But she also knew he was all bluster, and if called on it, would back down and charge a fair price or throw in enough extras to make up for the markups. His biggest problem was trying to make a job pay what he thought he deserved rather than what it was actually worth. This outlook let him believe he had the best of intentions.

Evan, on the other hand, had risen from real estate agent to broker as quickly as regulations permitted; then, for one reason or another, spent the next two years trying to talk EV into selling off large parcels of her land. First, there had been interest from a large entertainment company that wanted to build a theme park right on the line between Gilmore and Ponderosa Pines.

The residents of Gilmore had, for once, joined with their much-maligned neighboring town in an uproar against the proposal. As a result, it was squashed without even going to a vote when the conglomerate asked for a property tax waiver in addition to demanding major changes to the road system. The biggest hitch? They expected both towns to foot the bill.

Next, Evan approached one of the larger box stores and thought he had finally hit pay dirt until the owners demanded to be allowed a controlling vote to approve or disapprove any new business applications in a three-town radius.

Now he was behind the bid to combine the towns of Gilmore and Ponderosa Pines, and EV would have bet dollars to donuts he was playing both ends against the middle by telling the Gilmorians one story and Pines residents another.

If EV had not known the intimate details of his childhood, she would have seen the young man as something you scraped off your shoe after a visit to the dog park. Instead, she was well aware of how his mother had favored her eldest son, Luther—how she had held him up to Evan as the epitome of perfection while belittling her younger son, who soon began to turn bitter.

Even now, EV remembered young Evan as an earnest little soul with a sweet face and a love of animals. Over the course of a week, she had watched him charm and tame a feral cat that lived in the woods across from her house: a feral cat that she had been feeding for several months in the hope she could lure him close enough to catch with nothing to show for her troubles but some scored flesh.

All Evan had needed to do was sit quietly until the cat ventured from the shadowy forest depths and talk to it in a calm, clear voice. Each day the cat came closer as Evan poured out his love for the animal until, finally, the bedraggled feline lay purring in his arms. Never would she forget Evan's beatific expression as he petted the adoring cat, nor would she forget the look of sorrow on his face when he had to let it go.

His mother would never allow Evan to bring home a pet, but EV struck up a deal with the boy: if he could help her convince his gray-and-black-striped companion to move in with EV, then Evan could visit any time he liked. Mr. Tibbs had gone from a prowling tomcat to a lazy house pet who commanded the prime spot next to the fireplace for many years after Evan stopped visiting.

A measure of blame fell to her, in EV's estimation, for Evan having grown into the type of man he was today. At the time, she had been able to convince herself nothing would change, that her intervention might even make the situation worse. She suspected, now with hindsight, things had been worse at home than he had ever let on. In the face of his mother's obvious partiality to his brother, Evan's caring spirit tarnished and hardened until eventually he shut himself off from his one escape, EV. She could have stopped it but how do you explain to a boy that it was his face, the spitting image of his fathers, that reminded his mother of loss, not the boy himself?

That measure of blame EV placed on herself amounted to a fraction beside that heaped upon her by Evan.

As though her thoughts of him had conjured the man himself, Evan stepped out the coffee shop door to put himself right in her path.

"EV," contempt dripped from his tongue like honey from a honeycomb.

"Evan," EV sidestepped with the intention of walking past, but his hand shot out and grasped her forearm roughly. Pointedly, EV looked at his hand, then back at his face, her raised eyebrows telling him to let go more eloquently than words.

Slowly he complied. "I know what you did," he spat the words at her.

"Then maybe you'd like to enlighten me."

"My brother. You pushed him off that ladder."

Of course EV knew this rumor was circulating, but had dismissed the idea that anyone seriously believed it. Not for one minute did she believe Evan thought her a murderer. He had another game in mind.

Her level gaze met his. "I'm truly sorry for your loss, Evan; and, because I know you're grieving, I'm going to consider this an unfortunate outburst rather than the baseless accusation that it is."

"Baseless accusation? You argued with him in a public venue, then followed him to the church where a neighbor heard him fighting with a woman. Deny that."

Every single person in the place could hear the conversation through the screened door and at least two of them were surreptitiously typing away on their cell phones. Texting was the one place where EV's word of mouth grapevine and Chloe's electronic one intersected.

"Deny what? That Luther argued with a woman on the night of his death? If someone heard them, then it is an established fact. What proof do you have that I was the woman?"

"You argued with him at the meeting, who else would it be?"

"Oh, I don't know—his wife? Someone who was not happy with his work? One of the women who serve on the church board? It could have been anyone in town, but I can assure you it was not me."

"You killed him to stop me becoming mayor. You knew that with Luther dead, the incorporation meeting would be postponed, giving you time to kill the whole thing and become mayor yourself. You'd do anything to stop me finding out how you've singlehandedly controlled everything to do with Ponderosa Pines for years." Evan's voice escalated in volume until the last few words were shouted loud enough that the coffee drinkers could no longer feign ignorance. "You'd do anything to keep this place from growing into a normal town. Get out of the sixties, EV. Nobody wants to live in a commune anymore."

As though he had become aware of his audience and intended to convert them, Evan spoke in ringing tones, "Ponderosa Pines has unlimited growth potential. We need to expand our tax base, bring in outside money and business. The only one standing in our way is you, EV, with your provincial thinking. I'm the one who wants what's best, and I'm the one who can take this community and turn it into something."

Anger lit a fire in EV. "It's not the town that you want to elevate, but your own importance. Well, you can stop posing for that statue right now because it's never going to happen. I promise you I'll do whatever it takes to make sure that you," EV moved in close to poke Evan in the chest, punctuating her next words, "never."

Poke.

"Become."

Poke.

"Mayor."

With the final poke, she saw his eyes light with glee and knew she'd been played.

He wanted her to fight with him in front of witnesses, had maneuvered her into it with cunning and guile. All along he had known she was not the woman who argued with his brother, but now he had managed to plant seeds of distrust in the minds of some of the onlookers.

"This is not even close to over," she hissed.

Chapter 16

Whistling off key, Evan unlocked the door to his three-bedroom condo. As soon as the door closed out prying eyes, he took a victory lap around the kitchen island, circled back to gather the pile of mail lying on the welcome mat, and flicked on the lights. Nestled under a fragrant stand of the very pine trees the community had been named for, the brick building that housed his and three other identical but currently unoccupied units had a chalet feel to it.

Built during the '80's, High Acres was, as far as he knew, the only communally-owned apartment complex in the state—as an entity, the entire town owned and operated the clustered units. Rent payments went first to pay taxes and maintenance; anything left over was funneled into a communal fund that was currently earmarked for adding on to the complex.

Five brick structures now occupied the several acres surrounding a centrally located clubhouse facility that boasted free-to-use laundry facilities, a small but well-equipped gym, and an in-ground pool the entire town was welcome to use.

Rentals ranged from an incredibly cheap studio unit on the low end to considerably more expensive, top of the line units, in the newest building: three bedrooms, two baths, energy efficient appliances in a modern-looking interior that still managed to fall under the town's percentage of recycled materials. To look at the gleaming floors, you would never know their previous life had been as pallet boards. Even the brick exteriors were the cleaned and recycled remains of torn down buildings from when Warren updated parts of its town center.

In this goody-two-shoes of a sickeningly-sweet blot on the face of the earth, Acres was modern enough for Evan to feel he was living someplace almost normal.

When his cell pinged an incoming call, he checked the screen and saw it was his latest conquest. The woman was becoming tiresome. They'd had their day in the sun, and now it was time to move on; but she kept clinging, hoping for more than he wanted to give.

Letting boredom seep into his tone, he answered the call, "Hello," then rolled his eyes at the cooing of her voice in his ear.

"Please, stop calling. It's over. How many ways do I have to say it before you understand?"

A pause while she tried to convince him then, "No, I'm sorry; but I'm seeing someone else."

"You're the one who said it would be a fling, that you needed some excitement in your life."

The sobbing in his ear turned to accusation then to anger.

"I won't disagree with you; I am a jerk and a womanizer, but you knew that from the beginning."

"Yes, there's someone else and, yes, I was seeing her while I was seeing you. How can you be jealous when you're married?"

"Goodbye." He hung up the phone with a short laugh, "Guess that did it. Good riddance."

Evan leafed through his mail, pulled out one envelope, then tossed the rest carelessly onto the spotless, smoked-glass dining room table top. The sight of the by-now-familiar handwriting scrawled across heavy, cream colored paper turned a stomach already tender from tension into a bubbling mass of acid.

Sliding a finger under the flap, Evan managed to give himself a paper cut. Great, just the thing to top off a crappy day.

Blackmail.

Someone knew his deepest, darkest secrets and was using them against him. Three months ago, the first letter arrived with orders to perform a small task or watch his three most promising Gilmore real estate listings go up in smoke. He had ignored the letter and lost the listings. When the next letter arrived, Evan paid attention.

In no uncertain terms, the author laid out a laundry list of wrongdoing that Evan thought had been successfully covered up. The blackmailer had given him a limited number of days to convince the residents of Ponderosa Pines they wanted to be annexed by Gilmore, and his time was almost up.

Evan had spent the first week trying to figure out who had written the blackmail notes. It must be someone high up in Gilmore government who also had ties to Ponderosa Pines. If he didn't deliver, his biggest secret would hit the papers and his entire life would go down the tubes. No more license, no more real estate, no chance of ever becoming mayor.

If Luther hadn't gone and gotten himself killed, Evan might have had a shot at getting enough town members on board to make it happen. Why couldn't it have been EV who'd taken a header off a ladder? That would have solved all his problems.

For just a minute, he let himself miss his brother. Luther had always been his ball and chain—his weight to carry. Now that he was gone, taking with him his unconditional support, maybe he hadn't been quite as big a burden as Evan liked to think—maybe he even missed the big lug.

A frustrated flick of Evan's hand sent the envelope sailing. It was still fluttering downward when the heavy stone paperweight, taken from his own desk, crashed into the back of his head. Evan was dead before he hit the floor.

Chapter 17

Anyone who has ever lived in a small town knows that gossip can follow you down the street like a specter with its bony hand on your shoulder to pull it along. And worse, like that ghost, it never dies.

Not even when the gossip is complete lunacy.

Within hours of Evan's death, certain residents had already mentally tried and convicted EV of the murder—and without hearing any more evidence against her than that she had argued with him at a meeting and then again on the street.

Sleepy Ponderosa Pines had never known a crime spree of such epic proportions; two murders in under a month were having a profound effect on morale. One of the newest families was already talking about selling their home to move somewhere safer.

Tongues wagged, phones chirped, texts flew, and fingers tapped keyboards to create vast amounts of speculation. Anyone with a grudge against EV took the opportunity to embellish the lies so that by the next morning, two camps had formed with polar opposite opinions: both equally vocal, both aggressively fighting to sway anyone caught in the middle ground between them.

The first group, made up of level-headed, longtime residents declared her innocent while the second condemned EV as a hardened criminal mastermind corrupt enough to have been the fabled second gunman on the grassy knoll.

Ashton Worth was in the second group. He and his wife, Allegra, were relatively new to Ponderosa Pines, having moved there only eight years before. In a city neighborhood, eight years would have earned them dinosaur status; but small towns operate under an altered sense of time, which dropped them firmly into the sort of mid-grade category. Not quite new, yet not as trusted as a long-time resident.

Still, his middler status put him in a position where he had enough influence to sway the thinking of newer residents as well as those old timers in his immediate sphere of friends. So when he started speaking of EV's guilt as though it were an incontrovertible fact, people listened.

"I heard she's hated him ever since she caught him playing with one of her cats when he was just a boy," Ashton told a small group at The Mudbucket while he was getting his caffeine fix in a to-go cup for the drive into Gilmore.

Several times that day as he waited on customers from the Pines, he planted seeds of suspicion. "My wife saw her arguing with him the day before he died, and EV said she would do anything to stop him becoming mayor. Anything." With a knowing look, a nod of the head, an ominous tone of voice, he emphasized the word *anything*.

People listened and, worse, they repeated his words, his tone, and even the nod.

Some—the few residents who didn't like her to begin with— expanded on the theme, escalating it to ridiculous flights of fancy.

I heard she got those witch friends of hers to cast a spell on him. They danced naked under the full moon and cut the head off a live goat.

She swore revenge on him at the town meeting in front of God and everyone.

114

Someone said they saw her walking down the road with blood on her hands and a big smile on her face.

You know how everyone says Mr. Demetriou went into a nursing home? He's probably buried in her backyard.

Ashton started a few of the rumors himself, the others he perpetuated at every opportunity. Within 48 hours of Evan's death, half the newer residents were more afraid of EV than of global warming.

Millie Jacobs and Summer Beckett wasted no time leaping into the fray and upping the ante. Between them, they accused EV of everything from adultery to stealing chickens from every hen coop in town.

"The woman is absolutely depraved," Millie declared to anyone who would listen. "I know for a fact she's the one behind Marlene Burnsoll taking off out of the blue."

Everywhere she went, conversations ceased, people stared—or worse, refused to make eye contact.

None of that bothered EV as much as the looks of sympathy. She would rather be feared than pitied any day. Worse, all the speculation pushed at her stubborn nature; so, instead of keeping a low profile, she decided to spend more time out and about than normal.

The only people outside her closest circle of friends who treated EV normally were the town's children. Never having had any of her own, she tried to fill that gap in her life by going out of her way to spend time with other people's offspring.

Miz EV, as she came to be known, was popular among the younger crowd for the outrageous games she concocted for their amusement. One summer favorite was the annual fox and hound day she put on with Chloe; kids from ages six to sixteen were allowed to attend the all-day event.

Splitting into two groups, EV led the foxes in a loop through the town's forests and fields, leaving a trail for Chloe and the hounds to follow. At intervals, the older kids would branch off to lay a false trail, then double back to rejoin the group. With a half-hour head start, the foxes could only win if the hounds did not catch up to them before they got back to EV's house. At noon, wherever they were, both groups took a 45 minute lunch break and made their way to EV's backyard, where the whole game culminated in a cookout organized by the parents.

It was a summer highlight that might have to be canceled this year if nothing changed by the end of August unless she found a substitute leader for the foxes. This burden was weighing heavily on her mind when she ran into Horis walking toward her with a new shovel handle in his hand.

"Morning, EV." If Horis had heard the gossip, there was no evidence of such on his face. "Beautiful day."

Her eyes brightened at seeing the lack of guile in his. "Going to be another scorcher from the looks of things. You need any help out at the farm today?"

"Nothing special in the works, but an extra hand always makes the load lighter if you've a mind to stop by."

"Could I ask you a favor?"

"Sure, ask away." Affable as always, Horis grinned.

"Would you be willing to take over as fox leader this year if, you know, things keep going the way they are now? I'm *persona non grata* around here lately, and I wouldn't want to let the kids down. You know the woods as well as I do, and the kids all like you."

"It's not going to come to that; but, if it does, I'd be happy to do it."

EV grasped his arm giving it a squeeze of gratitude.

"Thanks, Horis. I knew I could count on you." Her words encompassed more than just the subject of foxes and hounds and turned his face red.

Despite her determination to carry on as though nothing had happened, the constant stress of wondering which of her neighbors was presenting only one side of their face had begun to wear on EV's nerves until she began finding excuses to avoid her usual daily outings.

Chapter 18

Almost everywhere EV went, conversation stopped or reduced to a whisper. Never mind that there was absolutely no physical evidence that she had ever been inside Evan's home or that, at the estimated time of death, EV had been visiting Thelma and Louise—no relation to the movie—better known as the Weird Sisters, in their tiny cabin on the outskirts of town.

Public opinion rated low on EV's list of worries, and she decided that not giving it any credence was the way to go. She would go on about her life like nothing was happening. True friends knew her propensity for violence was limited to a severe tongue lashing: mice left her home in a live trap to be loosed into the wild, spiders received the paper and cup treatment. EV was no killer. Even her gardens were geared toward repelling pests. She only killed as a last resort.

None of that changed a thing.

That EV found this more amusing than concerning had Chloe worried. Two brothers dead, both involved in a scheme that EV vocally opposed, and both dying within hours of that disagreement taking place publicly? Too much coincidence.

Chloe picked up her cell and speed dialed EV who answered on the first ring.

"Someone's trying to frame you."

"It's starting to look like a frame job." They both spoke at once.

EV chuckled but Chloe wasn't laughing.

"This is serious."

"Really? Because the way I see it, it's a comedy of errors. Think about it—how would Luther's death benefit me? There's no motive. At all."

"Well, I know that and you know that, but the killer might not."

A short pause while EV considered that. "True. Then who does have a motive?"

"See, that's where it all falls down. If the two deaths are connected, then Evan is no longer a suspect for killing Luther. Why would Talia kill Evan if they were doing the wild thing and one of them had already killed Luther because he was in the way?"

"Lover's spat?"

"I don't know her very well, but I always got the impression she kept Luther's danglies in her purse most of the time, and they were all over each other that night at the Yard. Unless that was just for show and she was trying to establish a cover. Or…maybe he was the one having an affair and she caught him." Chloe held the phone away from her ear when EV snorted loudly then dissolved into gales of laughter. "Okay, fine. I'll cross that theory off the list but I'm leaving Evan and Talia's affair on there for now."

Chloe added Talia and Evan's names to the mind map on her computer screen.

"Revenge for what, though? Luther bent over backwards to avoid confrontation. Could be a disgruntled worker. I know you're making one of your spreadsheet lists right now, I can hear the keys tapping. It's one line to tug."

"I've got a contact who would know the lay of the land; I'll do a little digging there." With a few deft motions, Chloe shot off a private message to a guy she'd dated once upon a time. Hopefully, he was hooked up or she'd end up feeling obligated to go out with him again. EV better appreciate the depths of her willingness to help.

"Annoyed homeowner? That's an easy list to put together, but I don't think we are going to find anything there. So that leaves money."

"No matter how I look at it, I have trouble thinking of anything Luther could have done that would get him murdered."

When Chloe murmured her agreement, EV continued, "Don't get me wrong; him falling off a ladder is no stretch to my imagination, but being pushed…that's an image I have trouble seeing."

"He's too stupid to live, but not smart enough to be killed?" There was no smile in Chloe's voice.

"Exactly."

"But, since we know Evan actually was being blackmailed, how does that figure in?"

"Only the dumbest blackmailer in history would kill their target." Every motive for the death of one brother contradicted the motive for the death of the other. Wasn't there some myth about a big snake who symbolized infinity by eating his own tail? That's what this felt like.

"What if Luther's death was spur of the moment? A crime of passion: he's arguing with whoever; they get pissed off, give the ladder a shove; down goes Luther; the killer panics and bolts."

Pausing, EV ran that scenario through her mind. That stepladder, she had reason to know, was rickety enough that shoving it over would have taken very little effort. Evan a small nudge could have toppled Luther. "It could have happened that way."

"Then we need to see if we can figure out who might have been there that night."

"How?"

"Social media for a start." Chloe switched her portable to speaker mode to free up both hands, and then opened up Facebook and Twitter. "You'd be surprised at the inane things people post on their profiles." Like a master pianist, she switched between her desktop, laptop, tablet and phone to look at images and posts dated on the fateful night. Fingers flying across the keys, Chloe began to establish a time line.

"No, I really, really wouldn't." Too many intimate details of people's lives being posted online for all to see was what kept EV from embracing social media.

"Okay," with one final rattle of keys, Chloe read off the names of her prime suspects, "we've got Lottie heading out to look for a stray cat, David Erickson was working late to finish up some painting at The Mudbucket and would have been on his way home around the time of Luther's murder, Allegra Worth was waiting for Ashton to get home so they could play Parcheesi—I wonder if that's a euphemism for…"

"I beg of you, don't finish that sentence," EV interrupted.

"Horis was out pouring beer in his slug bait containers. I think that's the short list of people who might have been at the church."

"Lottie despised Luther. There might be something there. I'm headed to knitting group. Wanna bet me it's packed and the topic of Luther will come up?"

"You are the queen of obvious. Call me after. I want details."

EV hung up.

Chapter 19

From the shape of her nose to her short, static way of moving to the habit of fluttering her hands when agitated, Priscilla Lewellyn really did have a bird-like quality that was only enhanced by her choice of clothing. Almost everything she wore was hand-knitted in her current favorite yarn: a novelty type that when stitched up created a garment that fell somewhere between fuzzy and feathery.

Yet, all that flutter and fluff concealed a mind sharp as a tack. Her eyes, beady as they might be, rarely missed a thing. Gossip was her passion, and her information was rock solid, which made her one of the taproots of the town grapevine.

So, it was with some reluctance, because EV was not an enthusiastic knitter and because she knew there would be fallout from the gossip about her, laden with needles and worsted yarn, EV set out to pay Priscilla a visit.

Priscilla's fabric store, Thread, occupied a spot between The Mudbucket—Ponderosa Pine's answer to Starbucks—and New Sage, a shop that carried an eclectic mix of goods ranging from hardware to health food to high-end kitchenware.

Lured by the scent of freshly roasted beans and the sight of Allegra Worth seated alone in front of the window, EV made an unplanned detour into the coffee shop to order a decaf latte. Since

Priscilla had banned food and drink from the fabric store, there was nothing for it but that EV plop down at the table next to Allegra's to sip her steaming brew.

Here was the closest source to the person spreading the most insidious of the EV-killed-Evan rumors, how could she pass up a chance to poke around a little?

"Shame about Luther and Evan. It's not often you see two brothers dying so close together. Would have killed their mother if she wasn't already gone." Only someone who was watching closely for a reaction would have seen Allegra's subtle flinch when she heard the two men's names.

Allegra swallowed hard and her voice, when she spoke, sounded hoarse. "Yes, it's so sad."

"You must have known Luther pretty well, growing up neighbors and all." EV relentlessly fished for information.

"Luther?" Allegra asked absently as though she had already lost track of the conversation.

"Didn't you date him before he married Talia? Must be a real shock to lose someone you were once so close to."

"What? Oh, yes. We dated in high school for a couple months or so."

"Evan would have been what—five or six at the time?" It was framed as a question, but EV knew exactly what the age difference was between the two brothers.

"Eight. He was eight when I was sixteen." A tear slipped down Allegra's face. "But age is relative, don't you think? After all, you're such close friends with that young neighbor of yours." She laid extra emphasis on the words *close* and *friends*.

Was she implying a romantic relationship between Chloe and EV? It almost sounded that way. EV grinned. Chloe was going to love this bit of gossip.

"Were you and Evan close friends?" EV kept her voice neutral. She appraised Allegra surreptitiously and saw a woman who was completely rattled. Fingernails once immaculately groomed were now chewed ragged, the polish a flaked ruin. Her makeup looked as though it had been applied with a shaky hand: there were mascara dots sprinkled beneath her lower lashes and her lipstick wobbled over her lip line. A glance down showed that though they were very similar, Allegra was wearing two different shoes.

The past few weeks had been hard on people of a certain temperament. With personal safety no longer a given, some folks struggled to maintain their equilibrium.

"Friends? Oh, no. I barely knew him."

Changing the subject, EV asked, "Are you coming to knitting group?"

At Allegra's blank look, EV simply pointed toward the reusable shopping bag stuffed full of yarn and needles hanging off the back of her chair. "Oh, I guess so." Yet, Allegra still sat like a lump of immovable rock until EV gently placed a hand around her arm and helped her to stand.

"We'll go together."

Stepping into Thread always jangled EV's nerves; so much color, so many patterns. It was a lot of visual stimulation and the main reason she had never taken up quilting as a hobby. With so many choices, her eye had a hard time landing anywhere. Cross stitching pushed against the extent of her patience for sewing things by hand. That lack of patience translated itself into her being the absolute worst knitter in the group. Even though she tried hard to make all her stitches the same, they inevitably bunched into tight knots and, when she tried to compensate, became a loose, flopping mess. Being the recipient of an item hand knitted by EV was more curse than blessing. Her crocheting skills, if possible, were even worse; and Chloe owned several parallelogram-shaped afghans to prove it.

The back room where knitting group met was a haven of restfulness compared to the front of the store. A slightly shabby, yet comfortable, sofa sat against the far wall beneath the only decorative element in the room: a beautifully wrought quilt depicting a map of Ponderosa Pines. Several equally threadbare chairs ranged around the rest of the room.

Taking recent events into account, EV expected the place to be packed and she was not disappointed. Chattering women filled every chair and were so crammed onto the couch that, had they bothered even trying to knit, the bumping of elbows would have clacked equally as loudly as their knitting needles. There was no pretense that this was anything but a gossip session. Only Priscilla sat calmly, fingers flying as a mitten formed below four small needles.

The others had been talking excitedly until EV stepped through the door and a flurry of motion erupted as hands delved into yarn bags to retrieve the projects that had ostensibly brought them here to begin with. EV, of course, was not fooled in the least and caught Priscilla's eye to exchange a wry smile.

Awkward silence continued until EV cleared her throat. "I take it you've all heard the rumor that I killed Evan." Her eagle eye circled the room to see which faces turned red, whose eyes slid away, and which of her friends exhibited indignation on her behalf. There were no surprises when it turned out that the former, thankfully smaller, group was also made up of those who did not regularly attend knitting group. Gossip seekers, every single one. Out of the corner of her eye, she saw Allegra flinch at the mention of his name.

With a wicked gleam in her eye, EV pulled out a folding chair, settled herself to face the room, and decided to set the cat among the pigeons. "What was my motive?" She ticked off possibilities on her fingers, "His little plan to combine Ponderosa Pines with Gilmore was never going to happen. I'm not the only one who was opposed to his becoming mayor; he had maybe five people in his corner on that. I wasn't sleeping with him; and, last I

126

knew, having a public fight with someone was not an automatic motive for murder."

EV reached down to pick up the knitting needle that had flown out of Allegra's hand at that last remark and calmly handed it back to the visibly flustered woman. "Any other ideas?"

Now she would get to the bottom of things and see what the grapevine had to offer.

"Of course you didn't kill Evan." Justice and Mercy Walker spoke as one; an eerie ability that came with being twins. Frankly, EV thought it was creepy that even in their thirties, they still dressed alike. Today, for instance, they were wearing identical hot pink tops over white leggings.

"So nice of you to be supportive," EV acknowledged, knowing full well the pair of them would assuredly have been among the top contenders if there had been a prize for who had spread the most rumors against her. Their part of the grapevine was twisted and stunted—probably from being coated in venom. "If I had decided to start pruning the unsavory element from our little community, Evan would not have been my first choice."

Mercy's eyes narrowed as though she thought that remark might have been aimed at her; but when EV kept her attention focused elsewhere, Mercy pasted on a cheery smile that did not reach her eyes. Then again, it might have been Justice; EV was sitting too far away to see the tiny mole just above her full top lip that marked one sister from the other. Either way, talking to one of them was pretty much the same as talking to the other.

"There ain't but three true motives for murder when you get right down to the bottom of it: love, money, or revenge." One of the newest Ponderosa Pines residents, Jessamyn Sanders, echoed Chloe's sentiments from their earlier conversation. She had pulled into the village one day on her Harley and, after wandering around for half an hour, declared herself home. Many eyebrows raised when she strutted into the rental office of High Acres and plunked down six month's rent plus security for a furnished one bedroom with an attached garage.

Hazel eyes alight, Jess continued, "And I'm thinking this time it was love."

"I believe you look like a cat who has just filled up on a nice canary dinner. Do tell." Priscilla's own eyes gleamed. She might as well have named her knitting group Priscilla's Gossip Club—Knitting Optional.

"Well, you know my place is just around the corner from his condo. Two days before he died, I happened to be walking in that direction, and I heard him having an argument with a woman," Jess's voice dropped to a whisper as she paused to let the full effect of this revelation sink in.

"Was it…" Allegra glanced toward EV, tried to cover up the quaver in her voice by clearing her throat. "Did you recognize the woman's voice?"

"No, it sounded like they were in Charlie Brown's teacher mode, but I could tell by their tones that neither one was happy."

Filing the information away in the must-tell-Chloe part of her brain, EV heard a sigh of relief coming from somewhere off to her right. Casting a sidelong look in that direction, she decided the most likely candidate was Luther's sister-in-law. Carlotta Calabrese was on EV's list of possible suspects based on Chloe's time line of the night Luther died and her opinion of the Plunkett brothers.

For once, though, Lottie remained silent. That, in and of itself, gave EV cause to bump her up the list.

Chapter 20

A lesser woman might have turned and walked away, considering the reaction EV was getting to her presence at Evan's funeral. Heads turned when she and Chloe walked into the church and whispers ran across it in waves. Among the expressions on her neighbors' faces were accusation, speculation, and sympathy.

All EV wanted to do was slip quietly into a seat in the back of the church; instead, Talia motioned for them to join her near the front where she had been saving a spot. Why had Talia chosen this very visible means of showing that she thought EV innocent of all wrongdoing? Was she trying to send a message? Judging by the look on Chloe's face, EV wasn't the only one who could have done without this particular vote of confidence.

There was nothing left for it, though, but that they march down the center aisle and take the proffered seats—so, with heads held high, that's exactly what they did. Still, Chloe made a mental note of who appeared to be supportive and which of their neighbors were scandalized. Some people were going to be eating crow before all this was over, and she wanted to make sure those who had earned it would get their full portion.

"Thank God you're here," Talia whispered, her sister Lottie nowhere in sight. "I was hoping you'd come so I wouldn't have to go through this alone." Was the woman completely oblivious to the gossip about EV? "You know I ended up having to make all the arrangements because Evan didn't have any other family."

"You did a great job," Chloe said, noting the fact that this funeral seemed like a Deja Vu version of Luther's: same casket, same flowers, same mourners. She wondered if Talia had gotten some kind of twofer discount. The feeling only intensified when the pastor began to speak and delivered almost the same eulogy for Evan as he had for Luther.

The two women exchanged a glance that plainly said they were freaked out by the whole thing.

Once the service was over, Talia clung to them like stink on a skunk.

"Don't leave me," the widow hissed in EV's ear when EV attempted to sidle away toward the classroom where a table held plate after plate of homemade sweets. Off to one side was another small table carrying the guest book and a slotted box for cards. This was where Lottie, under the guise of opening bereavement cards, had been hiding during the service.

Whatever feud was running between the sisters, the malevolent look she directed toward EV and Chloe hit like an arrow to the gut, and still wasn't as vicious as the one she shot toward Talia. It scorched the air between them like a bolt of lightning.

Unfortunately, when it hit it had an effect that Lottie probably never intended. Instead of being cowed, Talia's face flushed a dull red as she marched toward the table with her finger pointed. "I hope you're happy. You hated Luther even though he was a good husband to me. I think you hated him because of it," her voice rose toward shrill.

"Luther, Luther, Luther," Lottie wrinkled her nose with scorn. "That's all I've heard since you married that pathetic excuse for a man."

"What did he ever do to you?" The only other sound in the room was the nervous shuffle of feet while the crowd around them tried to decide between sneaking away or watching with blatant curiosity.

"Nothing, but then he never did anything for me either." Her words seemed pointed, but Talia stared at her sister uncomprehendingly.

"What on earth are you talking about?"

"My porch swing."

"You don't have a porch swing."

Lottie flashed Talia a raised eyebrow and a hand wave that spoke more eloquently than words.

"Let me get this straight: because Luther didn't build you a porch swing, you had to make my life hell for the past three years? And now that he's dead—DEAD—you can't even extend me the courtesy of some type of comfort?" With each sentence, Talia moved closer to her sister until she was poking Lottie squarely in the chest. The moment Lottie realized exactly how selfishly she was behaving, her mouth dropped open; but it was already too late.

"Get out," Talia growled. "Luther and Evan were my family, too."

"I'm sor..."

Talia held up a hand to stop Lottie from finishing.

"Don't. There's nothing you can say to fix this. Mark my words: from this day on, I have no sister."

Lottie's face fell, but she turned and walked away without trying to argue her side of the story.

Spinning back to face the crowd of people who were now making it a point to look anywhere but at her, Talia let her shoulders slump and then scrubbed a hand over her face before making a visible effort to shake it off.

Pointing to Priscilla Lewellyn, she asked, "Would you keep an eye on the food table for me?"

"Yes, of course." Even in the heat of late summer, Priscilla wore something knitted by her own hand. Today it was a loosely woven scarf in a subdued color draped across her slim hips, and a matching hat.

"EV and Chloe, if you would continue with what Lottie was doing with the condolence cards?" Talia raised her voice, "And the rest of you can just go ahead and text your friends who didn't come to let them know there was a meltdown at the funeral. Just get the gossip out of the way now so we can get on with burying the last of my family, such as it was."

She sailed out of the room to take her place near Evan's coffin while a chorus of voices assured her they would do no such thing. Yet, fingers still tapped out the tattoo to let texts wing their way toward interested neighbors, and the atmosphere in the church was charged with that undefinable excitement that goes along with scandal.

A look passed between EV and Chloe that spoke volumes before they did their part to set a good example for the rest of the town while knowing this topic would get a detailed discussion around the campfire that night.

On her way toward the table where the box of cards still sat, EV made it a point to gently jostle a couple of texters with a well-placed elbow, then follow up with a pointed look that resulted in phones being pocketed by their chagrined owners.

Only a handful of cards had been opened when Lottie had fled before her sister's ire. She had stuffed a couple checks and a ten-dollar bill into an envelope before noting the gifts on a small pad of paper. Falling into a rhythm, EV opened the cards then murmured the name and amount of any donation while Chloe took notes.

They were nearing the bottom when EV pulled out a business-sized envelope that felt and looked different from the others. "That's odd; this one is addressed to Luther. It's stamped, but not postmarked."

Chloe said dismissively, "Probably planned on mailing it then decided to come to the funeral instead."

But, when EV opened the envelope, instead of a card of condolence, she found a handwritten note. It was short and to the point.

I thought I had made myself clear. If you don't want all your dirty little secrets exposed, do what you were instructed to do. And soon. Or else.

"Look at this," EV hissed in Chloe's ear and handed the note over while looking around to make sure no one noticed.

Chloe's eyes widened then narrowed speculatively, "Well, that's interesting." She passed the note back to EV who slipped it back into the envelope which she folded and, turning away from the crowd, tucked into her bra.

"You're not going to show that to Talia?"

"Not right now. She's distraught, though it doesn't feel like a woman mourning a lover. I'm starting to think she's exactly what she seems to be. I think we need to keep this quiet until we can figure out who actually was banging Evan on the side."

"Nice language for a woman your age," Chloe teased.

EV snorted, "I haven't been fitted for orthopedic shoes just yet."

Chapter 21

Under an angry dark sky that didn't just threaten rain but promised it, EV and her prey crossed paths on the sidewalk in front of Thread, which saved her from having to seek him out. Dressed in civilian clothes, the deputy carried a ridiculously large blue-and-white-striped umbrella.

"You figure out who killed Evan and Luther yet, or do you still think I did it?"

"Well, good morning to you, too."

"Yeah, yeah, good morning. Now, spill. Have the autopsy results come back from the coroner's office?

"Now, Emmalina, you know I can't divulge information about an ongoing investigation."

"Call me *Emmalina* again and we'll be investigating your death next, Earnest Dalton Burnsoll." EV smiled to take the sting out of the words. Very few people ever used her given name—and none of them were forgiven for doing so—but alienating her best source of information was not a solid plan.

"Okay, EV. I take your point." Having also been named by parents from the peace and love generation, he was no more enamored of the name Earnest than she was of *Emmalina* and went by *Dalton*. *Deputy Earnest* didn't quite have the same ring as *Deputy Dalton* did. Not that he had been using that particular moniker for very long.

Dalton, at loose ends after selling his coffee shop to that nice young Erickson couple, badgered Nate into deputizing him just to keep himself busy. The job paid almost nothing, which was more than Dalton needed anyway, and he was finding the investigation fascinating. Nearly as fascinating as EV herself.

"Come to dinner with me, and I'll bring along the crime scene photos."

"You mean like a date?"

"Exactly like a date."

His interest came as no surprise to EV who refused to consider him in that way. She liked men well enough and took one home when she was in the mood, but she was strictly a catch-and-release kind of woman. Dalton was not the throw-him-back type, though. She could almost smell the settle-down on him.

Taller than her by a couple inches, Dalton's love of hiking kept him physically fit. Thick, dark hair curled softly at his collar with only touches of gray at the temples giving away his age. Dark eyes framed by a few crinkling laugh lines gazed at her with the barest hint of a twinkle.

Just look at him, standing there all hopeful. Telling him no would be like kicking a puppy. Getting a look at those photos might be worth an awkward evening. He'd just better not try to kiss her. That would complicate things a lot. Especially if she liked it as much as she suspected she might.

"Fine. Pick me up at seven and don't forget those photos."

EV brushed past him before he could see the satisfied smile on her face. If she played it right, he would be feeding her all the information she needed. If she had looked back, she would have seen him staring after her with a similar expression.

* * *

136

As 7:00 pm approached, EV found herself wrestling with the urge to strangle her best friend with a nylon stocking. "This skirt," Chloe pulled a tiered skirt in a vibrant southwestern-style print from where it had been shoved into the depths of the closet, "with this," followed that with a softly knit turquoise top, "these shoes," white sandals that EV didn't ever remember buying, "and now for the jewelry."

"For the love of tiny pickles. It's just a fact-finding mission, not a real date." All the protest netted her was a raised eyebrow and a cheeky grin. "Fine," she grumbled, "tart me up like a prized turkey and send me off to the slaughter."

"It's a frigging date, EV. Go, eat, dance or something. Have fun." Chloe ignored all protests and, before she knew it, EV was dressed and ready. Her hair, a lovely shade of sable with only a few strands of silver starting to show, was tucked behind ears adorned with silver hoops. A chunky silver necklace studded with moonstones lay gently on the modest neckline of the turquoise top Chloe had forced her into, and a matching bracelet circled her wrist.

"You look amazing. Dalton's going to freak." Gently, Chloe turned EV toward the full-length mirror tacked on the back of her bedroom door. EV had to admit: she did clean up well.

"Jerk blackmailed me into it. He'd better have those photos." What in hell was that nervous flutter in her belly?

Get hold of yourself, you're long past feeling like a teenager.

"Shush, he's here." Chloe heard the slam of a car door and peeked out the window. "He looks pretty hot. Now go. I'll let myself out." She wagged a finger at the older woman, "You be nice to him. It wouldn't hurt you to have a man in your life."

"Pots should not be pointing fingers at kettles of the same color." EV sailed down the stairs then whisked the door open to find Dalton standing on the step with a grin on his face and one hand behind his back.

"You'd better have those photos back there and not something cheesy like flowers or candy." Social situations like this always made EV feel awkward. Feeling awkward made her surly. Feeling surly made her feel awkward. It was a vicious circle.

In her mind, her rangy body and six feet of height morphed into a mass of nothing but knees and elbows that bent every which way. There was no way she would ever fit into the crook of a man's arm like those dainty, petite women with curves always seemed to do. Never mind that she found those tiny, giggling damsels annoying beyond all measure; they were what every man wanted. Oh, she could have a man in her bed any time she wanted, but sex and romance were leagues apart, in her opinion. Sex was fun and easy; romance was a quagmire that could suck a woman in, then take her down to hell and leave her with nothing. That much she knew from experience.

The nasty snipe made not so much as a dent in Dalton's smile; if anything, it became wider and more cheerful. "I know better than to try and woo a woman like you with anything so trite as flowers or candy; give me some credit." From behind his back, he pulled a stone: perfectly oval granite, pink flecked, flattened and smoothed by the surf he'd picked it out of during his last visit to the east coast. The minute he had seen it, the stone had reminded him of EV. "I thought you could use this in your rock garden."

From her vantage point at EV's bedroom window, Chloe had to suppress the urge to whoop. A man who knew her friend well enough to realize a hunk of granite meant more to EV than a diamond might just manage to drill through that cranky exterior to the strong, vital, caring woman underneath.

EV's mouth opened, then closed again. Blast the man for putting that flutter in her belly with nothing more than a pretty rock. She reached out to take it from him, ran her hands over the water-smoothed surface while the blush faded from her face. "Thank you, Dalton; it's beautiful." She was already picturing the garden cairn she would build with this as the peak.

When he gently pulled the stone from her grasp, the brush of his fingers against hers sent up another little tingle that reminded her it had been long months since she had taken a man to her bed. Didn't matter, though; Dalton would never make her list of willing playmates. He was not the kind of man who played slap and tickle lightly.

Too earnest.

Hah, nice play on words there; Earnest was too earnest.

While this nonsense chased itself through her head, Dalton eased EV into his car and backed out of the driveway in the opposite direction to the one she expected him to take.

"Where are we going?"

"Well, I'm not going to whip out those crime scene photos right in the middle of The Mudbucket; so I figured we'd go incognito. Maybe drive over to Warren, find a little pub or a diner where no one knows us."

"Can't blame you for not wanting to be seen with me. After all, I'm Nate's prime suspect. Wouldn't do for people to think we're in cahoots. Next thing you know, you'll be on his list, too."

"For Pete's sake, EV; nobody with half a brain thinks you bashed Evan over the head or shoved foolish Luther off a ladder."

"That's not true, and you know it. Ashton Worth swears he saw me leave the church, and Mercy keeps telling everyone and their neighbor she heard Luther arguing with a woman. That's pretty damning evidence even if it's anecdotal. Add in the fact my fingerprints are all over the ladder—never mind that I used it when I swapped all the light bulbs in the church over to the LED type just last month—and I'm surprised every day I don't wake up in the pokey."

"Ponderosa Pines is one of those places where, when it comes to gossip, one plus one equals six."

"Just the nature of the beast; every time a story's told, someone puts their own spin on it." With a wicked gleam in her eye and a twist of her lips, EV elaborated, "You remember the story of how two local teens were caught skinny dipping in Singing Creek and how there's barely any truth to it at all."

The barb missed its mark entirely. "Oh, there was truth and plenty of *barely* to go along with it. We were seventeen, in love, and naked."

"What happened between you two?" One of the few mysteries in Ponderosa Pines was the reason Marlene Burnsoll had left her husband. Both versions of the grapevine had been uncharacteristically mum on the details. Silence stretched between them until Dalton finally broke it by saying, "I'm surprised you don't already know. Aren't you pretty high on the gossip chain?"

"Oh, Sweetie, I'm the crucial link; but anything you tell me in confidence will never pass these lips."

His eyes glanced away from the road to quickly search hers to assure himself she was telling the truth. Once he was convinced, he cleared his throat.

"Marlene fell out of love with me."

"Was there someone else?"

"There was."

"Where did she meet him?"

"Her. Marlene reconnected with her at their twenty-year class reunion last February."

"Ah. Well, I'm sorry—for what it's worth. Marlene isn't the love-'em-and-leave-'em type. Can't see her intentionally setting out to hurt you."

Dalton stared straight ahead. "No, she struggled with it for months before she told me. I want her to be happy."

"You're a good man, Earnest Dalton Burnsoll." EV reached out and laid a sympathetic hand on his knee. When his face burned red, she realized he might have taken it for more than the gesture it was and snatched her hand back like his leg was on fire.

"And what about you, Emmalina Valentina Torrence? Are you the love-'em-and-leave-'em type? How is it you're still single?"

"Oh, you know me. I'm a social butterfly, flitting from flower to flower but never lighting in any place for too long." It was a warning that any attempt to become romantically attached to her would not end well for him.

Pulling into the parking lot of Little Bill's diner saved Dalton from the backlash he would surely receive if he had uttered any one of the number of retorts that sprang to mind. It's a smart man who knows when to shut up and cut his losses.

Finally, after what felt like an eon to EV, she was swallowing the last morsel of an unexpectedly well-cooked steak. Little Bob knew his way around a sirloin.

Every time Dalton tried to turn the conversation personal, EV trotted out another bit of ridiculous town gossip to keep him distracted; and whenever his gaze turned warm, she deflected by asking about his family. And still, he dragged their time together out for as long as possible by pressing dessert on her. But, since it turned out Little Bob also had a way with blackberry pie, EV let him slide until the last bite of flaky crust tinted dark with berry goodness was gone.

Then, when Dalton did not immediately pull out the photos, EV folded her arms and gave him her best stink-eye.

"I held up my end of the bargain; now it's your turn," she pointed her finger and tapped it on the table. "Consider it an intermission from the date portion of the evening."

"Agree to go dancing with me on Friday and I'll even let you look at the preliminary coroner's report."

Regardless of the way she saw herself, EV never lacked dating opportunities. There were more eligible bachelors in Ponderosa Pines than single women, but that wasn't what drew men to her. Something about her independent nature challenged them to try and tame it, which was exactly what repelled her the most.

Leaning back in her seat, she tilted her head and studiously considered Dalton. Smart, funny—she ticked of the pros in her mind—didn't puff out his chest like a Neanderthal or talk down to her, not bad looking. Then the cons—divorced less than a year, likely to want something more serious than her usual roll-in-the-hay-then-call-it-a-day type of relationship.

"What kind of music would we be dancing to and when do I get to see the report?"

Now it was his turn to consider her. Picturing her in cowboy attire doing some type of two-step or line dance seemed all kinds of wrong. Ditto for swing. He ventured a guess, "Hard rock, and you can see the report right now."

"Done." She circled her hand impatiently for him to hand over the photos and report while he tried to hide a grin behind one hand and use the other to rifle through the messenger bag hanging over the back of his chair. When he finally pulled out a tablet and switched it on, EV was getting close to the end of her patience. Resisting the urge to bounce in her seat, she watched him tap open a folder and finally got her first look at how Luther had died.

Without thinking, she pulled the tablet across the table and spun it so she could see better, then began flipping through the images. Luther lay with feet tangled in the bottom rung of the ladder, head twisted at an unnatural angle, and unseeing eyes staring straight ahead. Whoever had taken the photographs had captured the scene from every direction. EV flipped through them twice before closing the file and opening the one labeled with Evan's name.

When the first image sharpened into view, EV's eyes widened before she turned away, swallowed hard to dislodge the lump in her throat, and hoped she wouldn't embarrass herself by throwing up on the table. Not even the biggest jerk in the world deserved to die like that.

Dalton reached across the table intending to pull the tablet away from her, to close the folder and hide the stark images where they could no longer put sadness into her eyes.

"No," She stopped him, "I need to see. People are saying I did this; I need to know what they think I'm capable of."

When she looked a second time, the blood seemed less shocking—less vividly red where it matted and clumped in his hair then spread across the floor. Next to his head lay the murder weapon. A heavy stone paperweight.

Slowly she paged through each image while Dalton watched the emotions play across her face: sorrow, sympathy, anger, and lastly resolve. With a short, angry motion, she shoved the tablet toward him, "Open the report," when he paused, she added, "Please," in a softer tone.

He complied then excused himself to visit the restroom. The second he was out of sight, EV's fingers flew over the touch screen while keeping an eye out for his return. Just because she hated these little devices didn't mean she couldn't use one when she had a need. Within seconds, a copy of everything was winging its way to Chloe's email.

* * *

The telltale *beep-boop-boop-beep* of Chloe's phone indicated a new email had arrived, and her eyes widened as she scrolled through the files forwarded from Dalton's tablet. Peeking at the clock on her bedside table she noted that it was after 11 o'clock at night. *Good for Dalton*, she thought. *He made her partake in an entire date before handing over the goods.* Chloe was already snuggled into bed, and refrained from trudging up to her office for a better look on her computer screen and instead grabbed her tablet from the charging port nearby.

Further inspection sobered Chloe's mood, and as she scrolled through the crime scene photos she shuddered at the thought of one murder happening so close to home, much less two. One of the skills she learned in journalism school was how to remain detached from unpleasant images, but it was a whole lot easier when you

143

didn't know the individuals involved. The sight of empty eyes on a face you were used to seeing full of light and animation was unsettling, and could make even the most stoic person in the world wary of her own mortality.

In addition to the photos, EV had forwarded the preliminary coroner's report and an image of a drawer full of handwritten note cards. Chloe didn't have to use her investigative skills to conclude that these must be the blackmail letters written to Evan. Judging by the number of envelopes, the extortion had been going on for quite a while. Whatever was in those envelopes might hold the key to finding out who had killed the Plunkett men. They needed more information, and there was only one place they were going to get it. It was time for an honest conversation with Nate, and only a small part of her, buried deep down was looking forward to it for reasons other than helping solve the murders.

Chapter 22

August continued, hot and sticky, as it always did, and Ponderosa Pines was at a near standstill save for the poor souls on farm duty rotation. Everyone else typically adopted a South American attitude toward the weather, choosing to relax on the pond and take mid-day siestas until the cool breezes of September rolled in.

Aiming a portable misting fan at the back of her neck, Chloe meandered toward town for some iced coffee. *It will be winter soon, enjoy the warm weather while it lasts,* was Chloe's mantra. In a few months, she would be wishing it was warm again, but at this moment the thought of cool, crisp autumn air sounded like heaven.

Outside The Mudbucket, several patrons languished on the brick patio. Some carped about the heat while others cast irritated glances toward the window, where the business end of an air conditioner dripped and hummed loudly. It wasn't much cooler inside, but she imagined the wait staff appreciated the slight reprieve.

"Three large iced coffees with cream please. And some sugar on the side." Chloe answered the damp-looking barista when she barked out a cranky "What'll it be?" She took no offense, chalking up the attitude as heat-related. "Oh, and a dozen glazed donuts."

Okay, the eye roll wasn't necessary, but Chloe brushed it off, and congratulated herself on remembering that Nate couldn't resist the moist, yeasty dough bombs.

When Dalton sold the shop, he included his famous recipe—a gesture much appreciated by the entire town. Everything tasted pretty much the same across the board, but the Ericksons had added their own unique flair to the menu. Several varieties of smoothies, a couple of homemade soups, and veggie wraps to die for had turned the Mudbucket from a simple coffee shop into a popular lunch spot.

The aforementioned patio was an excellent spot for people watching, and since everyone in town was a busybody in one way or another, the outdoor area was usually considered the best seat in the house. Chloe knew EV preferred her perch by the kitchen door, but the patrons sitting outside were particularly loose-lipped. Today, however, the entire town was only talking about one subject, and Chloe didn't hear anything she hadn't heard already.

A short walk along a well-beaten path through a patch of apple trees led Chloe to the Pines' small municipal building. Positioned kitty-corner from the Grange Hall, the octagon-shaped structure held a couple of small offices utilized by the current select men and women, and a part time clerk who handled fishing and hunting licenses and collected excise tax for vehicle registrations. Though not entirely necessary, the town provided their resident Deputy with an office located in the back of the building. Chloe wandered around to use the dedicated entrance.

Resistance met her tentative push on the office door. Peering around the box of donuts she balanced precariously on top of the tray of iced coffees, Chloe pushed harder and nearly fell in a heap onto a pile of file boxes.

A frazzled looking Dalton took the box of donuts from her so suddenly that the absence of weight threw her into another near spill. She glared at Nate, who's mouth was screwed up into a mischievous smile he was obviously trying to disguise as concern.

"Why don't you take your coffee and donut outside, and find a shady place to eat, Dalton? It's time for a break, and it's probably no hotter out there than it is in here." Nate suggested.

"OK, boss. Nice to see you, Chloe." Dalton nodded to her, looking slightly disappointed at not being allowed to listen in on Chloe and Nate's impending conversation. "How's EV doing?" he added with a hopeful look.

"She could be better, Dalton. Everyone in town thinks she's Satan on a stick." Chloe replied with a sarcastic roll of her eyes. "Why don't you call her, I think she could use some support, much as she'd hate to admit it." She relented after seeing the crestfallen look cross his face.

Once he departed Chloe took a seat across from Nate and peered around the room. A distinct mark in the middle of the carpet matched the pattern of Nate's desk legs. The desk was now pushed against one wall, presumably to make room for Dalton's workspace.

Mismatched shelving lined the back office wall, and held a potpourri of items ranging from political science textbooks to fingerprinting and office supplies. She spotted a dusty bottle of antacids and one of those mounted talking fish among the mishmash.

Boxes piled high next to the door were labeled with dates, and Chloe remembered that all town records had been kept in this office behind a giant locked filing cabinet. It seemed to have disappeared in favor of Dalton's desk. Every surface was covered with stacks of brown folders in various states of disintegration.

"Nice mess, huh? It was my bright idea to make Dalton a deputy. He seemed so eager, and having a helping hand sounded genius. But it seems I've created more work for myself in the form of organizing thirty years of town records. Do you know what kind of ridiculous documents were saved by the elders? I don't care that in 1988 you purchased two cases of staples! Records retention was definitely a concern. So what's going on, and why did you bring me high cholesterol?" Nate ranted until Chloe frowned directly at him with her right eyebrow raised.

"Wow, Mr. Crankypants. Tell me how you really feel!"

"I know you're not here just for the pleasure of my conversation, or to fatten me up with donuts. What do you want?" Chloe liked *friend* Nate more than she liked *cop* Nate, that was for sure. She hoped he would settle in soon and lose the 'tude. As much as he didn't want to be here, Chloe thought he was acting like a big baby about the whole situation.

"I want to see the blackmail notes you found in Evan's things." Chloe responded without hesitation.

Nate allowed his mouth to drop open for a split second before snapping it shut again. "How do you manage to know as much as a trained detective? And how am I supposed to conduct an official investigation with everyone in town sticking their noses in where they don't belong?"

"Might as well accept it; there's nothing you can do about it. We heard it first from Lottie—and you know if there's something to dish she's going to make sure the whole town eats it up."

He sat back and surveyed Chloe, his countenance morphing from disbelief and irritation to one of mischief and curiosity. "What are you going to give me in return?" His eyebrow rose in perfect imitation of Chloe's earlier expression.

Unsure whether he was flirting with her or not, several thoughts—and a thrill of excitement—raced through Chloe's head as she prepared a response. *Is the entire Ponderosa Pines police force unopposed to bribery as long as it involves scoring a date?* But since Nate had never asked her and been turned down, she chalked his attitude up to facetiousness and replied calmly, "I happen to also know that Luther received at least one threatening note of his own. I have the original, and I will give it to you as evidence. I don't know if there were more; and I'm not exactly in a position to ask, since I don't know if Talia's aware of the situation. I don't want to put any more on her plate right now. In addition to the note, EV and I will give you the inside scoop on all the Ponderosa gossip you can stomach."

Digesting the information Nate opted not to scold Chloe again. At least she had come to him directly, and not sat on that note. He knew she was trustworthy, even if impetuous, and he could see there was no equal to the quantity and quality of EV and Chloe's knowledge when it came to town affairs. Plus, working closely together had its perks. First off, he could make sure she didn't get into trouble. Secondly, maybe he would finally get the opportunity to find out if she was interested in him as more than a friend.

A smile flitted briefly across his face before Nate turned serious, "I want you to stay out of trouble and keep me in the loop. You want in on this: you have to be up front with me and you have to promise that you won't do anything *Chloe*-like. You share with me; I'll share with you. Let's just get these murders solved so I can finish cleaning this hell-hole office and things can get back to normal. Or as normal as things ever are here in *Brigadoon*."

Chloe considered. "I can agree to that. At this point we're trying to figure out who Evan was hooking up with, and whether or not the blackmail had anything to do with either his or Luther's death. I really thought it was Talia he had his sights on, but now that Evan's dead it doesn't make sense." Possibilities began to swirl around in her head once more, but Nate cut her off.

"It wasn't Talia or Evan who killed Luther. I'm sure of it. He had an alibi, and I could tell from Talia's reaction that it wasn't her. I can't be positive she and Evan weren't having a relationship, but I can tell you she didn't kill her husband."

Nate looked concerned and continued, "We also haven't found any other evidence that Luther was being blackmailed; we only found notes addressed to Evan. I haven't been able to pinpoint a solid motive for killing Luther. Maybe this is it."

His tone was hopeful, not frustrated, as Chloe expected it to be, considering he was being clued in on an important piece of evidence that he hadn't been able to ferret out himself. But ultimately, Nate was a realist and a good detective. He considered any evidence welcome—regardless of the source—especially around the mid-point of a seemingly dead-end investigation.

"We can't rule out the possibility that he did receive other threatening letters. This one certainly makes it sound like the extortion was ongoing. Maybe he hid them somewhere." Chloe suggested.

She handed Nate the blackmail note addressed to Luther and within minutes was duplicating the entire Plunkett file page by page on an old dinosaur photocopier Nate inherited when the municipal office purchased a newer model. Placing the lot in a shiny new brown folder Chloe vowed to text EV as soon as she left the office.

Chapter 23

EV's small dining room looked like a serial killer's bedroom with crime scene photos plastered to the walls, and files spread out over the table. A white board was stationed at one end of the room, covered in various notes and speculations; the only thing missing was tack-covered map criss-crossed with string to indicate the killer's movements.

Both EV and Chloe were poised over copies of the blackmail notes found in Evan and Luther's belongings. It certainly looked as though someone, tired of their subterfuge, had decided to cash in on whatever misdeeds the men thought were long buried. Intending to study every detail of the police file and attempt to fill in the blanks, they were meticulously re-reading the notes for at least the 20th time. In all the passing back and forth, the documents had gotten shuffled out of order.

"Let's lay them out in order, and separate everything according to whether it corresponds with Luther or Evan." EV suggested. Another five minutes of staring and a look of understanding crossed her face.

"Do you see what I see?" EV asked Chloe with a raise of her brow.

"There's something off. What is it?"

"It's the handwriting. The wording is similar, but look at the way the *A*'s are off-center with a diagonal slash in Luther's notes."

"The *S*'s are different too; there's more flourish on the Evan notes. What do you think this means? A blackmailer with some type of alternate personality disorder? Two different blackmailers; one forging the notes from the other? Or, only one blackmailer, and someone trying to make it look like two?" Chloe sighed and followed the logical conclusion. "And then, if only one brother was actually being blackmailed, which one was it?"

Noticing that both coffee cups were empty, the two migrated into the kitchen for a refill. Chloe hopped up to sit on her favorite corner of EV's counter top.

"There's a solid argument for either of them being the actual target. Evan's life was filled with nothing but dark corners, but Luther swindled a lot of people out of money. It's possible someone wanted to get back what was rightfully theirs. Plus, they were both in on the proposal to the town board, even if Luther was the one to broach the subject."

"We can't rule out the fact that Luther may have received more notes. And I think it's a safe bet to say that whoever wrote the fake notes has to be the killer. Which means at least one of the deaths isn't about the blackmail at all; it's about something else. But what else connects them besides their asinine plan to merge with Gilmore, and the fact that they're brothers?"

"Well, we've already ruled out anything to do with Talia. Because she wouldn't kill Luther so she could be with Evan, and then turn around and kill him, too. That's just stupid." EV nodded her agreement.

"But, I saw her with Evan; that scarf has to be the only one of its kind in Ponderosa Pines. Unless I misread the situation." Chloe stared into space, recalling the moment she laid eyes on Evan and the mystery woman. "Even Nate will tell you that conversation they were having at Mama Nancy's was intimate. Not a brotherly bit of condolence, either. They were giving off the *we're-getting-ready-to-do-it* vibe." She shuddered at the thought.

"We're missing something." EV began pacing the floor, walking all the way around the kitchen island, turning on her heel and walking back the other way. "Unless Evan killed Luther, and Talia killed Evan out of revenge, all of this adds up to a dead end."

"Do you think we should confront Talia? See if we can pry something out of her about her relationship with Evan? If they were doing the nasty, she might be the key to everything. Plus, she's always so fidgety. It makes me suspicious."

"I don't know. Talia's always been that way; she has a lot of nervous energy. What's more, if we confront her, it will tip our hand. Give it a day or so; something will come through the grapevine, it always does. What about your digital gossip channel? Any gems of info we can mine?"

"It's been suspiciously quiet with the bits and bytes lately."

"I've had fewer sources myself since I landed on the hot seat as suspect number one." Bitterness crept into her tone, "I'm learning a lot about my 'true friends'. Like which ones have been tearing me down behind closed doors because they think I won't find out."

Chapter 24

Somewhere in the background, Chloe could hear a bell ringing. She bolted upright and searched all around through half-closed lids, trying to figure out what was making the blasted noise, while simultaneously blocking the sun from boring a hole through her eye sockets. She tried swiping across her cell phone screen, then moved on to the digital alarm clock resting on her night stand.

After pressing each button several times, she resorted to yanking the cord out of the wall socket with a violent jerk. When the shrieking ended, Chloe fell back onto her pillow and heaved a sigh. Her plan to get up early and bang out this week's column had seemed like a good idea when she set the alarm last night. If it hadn't been for the fact that her best friend's name was being dragged through the mud she would have happily snuggled in for a few more hours' sleep.

The scent of fresh coffee curled around her nose and pulled the corners of her mouth up into a smile. Chloe gave herself an imaginary pat on the back for having the foresight to set the timer along with her alarm clock the night before. A few moments later, she settled herself onto a kitchen bar stool with a steaming cup of dark roast and a bowl of Greek yogurt topped with honey.

She ran the tip of her tongue through a layer of creamy yogurt until it met the resistance of thick, smooth honey, enjoying the juxtaposition of two dissimilar, but pleasantly compatible, sensations. When she had licked the last spoonful clean and rinsed her bowl, Chloe headed upstairs to get to work.

Too many emails were waiting in the Cone's inbox, and Chloe sifted through several before she noticed the one from Technical Support. The tip line voicemail box was finally working again; since she hadn't been able to access the messages for close to three weeks, it was sure to be a long and interesting morning.

Chloe opened the bottom drawer of her desk, pulled out an old brick-red lock box, and removed a thick leather-bound ledger from inside. The phrase *Busybody Central* had been stamped across the front cover, and Chloe could hear Wesley's sing-song voice answering the Cone's dedicated line with the same phrase. She transcribed every tip received that day, as she always did, including as many details as possible in case she needed to refer back at a later date.

The first two messages were obviously from either Justice or Mercy Walker, who had tried but failed to disguise an unpleasant, nasal whine. Both messages were aimed at implicating EV in Luther and Evan's murders, but as they stated only suspicion and absolutely zero details she could follow up on, Chloe pressed 7 to delete them.

She was nearing the end of her patience for nonsense when something about the next caller's voice caught her attention. A whispering voice that Chloe recognized as female stated simply: "Mr. Worth's word isn't worth much. I know for a fact he was catting around near the church on the night Luther Plunkett died."

While it wasn't a terribly detailed message, the fact that a name besides EV's was being thrown out as a possible suspect came as a welcome change. Chloe added Ashton to her list of names for investigation, saved the message in case she needed it later, and continued through the voicemails until all were either archived or permanently deleted.

Flipping through the ledger before putting it back into its box, Chloe recalled her first week at the *Pine Cone*. Wesley had given

156

her this book, and sent her to his attic library to read old editions of the newsletter. After a solid seven days of finding Chloe curled up there in the morning, sound asleep with her nose in a pile of papers, Wesley insisted she go home and write her own column. It had been, for the most part, smooth sailing since then. But writing about actual murder was a lot different from reporting that Mavis Cooter had been given an unfortunate eyebrow wax at the *Hootchie Cootchie Salon.*

It wasn't long before Chloe was tapping away at the keyboard, funneling her frustration into her column.

Hey, Piniacs, are you ready to dish? Which town matriarch is being put through the ringer by her own friends and neighbors? And, what pair of viscous sisters tried to implicate her via the Pine Cone's automated tip line? Maybe it's time to bark up a different tree, people!

On a lighter note, which bespectacled farmer found a couple of randy teenagers necking in his hayloft last Friday night? Parents, do you know where your children are?

Could a certain pair of twins be on the outs? Word has it the two were spotted, suspiciously wearing differing outfits for the first time in…forever! What could split the gruesome twosome in half? I have a theory—I just hope someone warns the poor guy before it's too late.

And last but not least, ladies, how happy are you that Inspector Hottie is back in town? Will you sleep easier knowing he's watching over you, or will the thought just keep you up at night?

Chapter 25

"Ow," Chloe sucked her thumb where a cucumber spine had jabbed into it. She scrunched up her nose and winged the soon-to-be-pickle into the basket at her feet with force. "You bring another pair of those gloves? These things bite hard."

"Over there with my water bottles." EV nodded and kept on picking.

"Remind me again why we volunteered to spend half a day bent over harvesting cucumbers when it's hotter than a picnic in hell?"

"We," EV emphasized, "volunteered because YOU are addicted to pickles. You got that from your mother. She never met a gherkin she didn't like."

"Why is it always my fault?"

"Whippersnapper so you are." EV intoned.

"Thanks, Yoda," Chloe deadpanned.

"Just keep picking; you'll thank me later when you're sucking down my special mustard spears. The ones I make from my grandmother's recipe."

"Which you refuse to give me."

"I ever tell you about my grandmother and her recipes?"

Chloe loved hearing stories about EV's family. "No, I don't think so."

"Well, she calls them *receipts* and if she deigns to give you one, she writes it out herself so she can alter the ingredients just a little. Not enough to totally screw up the dish, but just enough so yours won't taste exactly like hers. When she gave me the pickle recipe, she doubled the amount of alum in it so my first batch was horrific."

"How did you figure it out?"

"Sneak attack. I waited until she went to sleep, and rifled through stacks of recipe cards and little scraps of paper until I found it. Remind me to make her prize winning blueberry cake sometime. Snagged that one, too, and found out she substituted nutmeg for cinnamon."

Half an hour later, sweat running in her eyes, EV announced a water break and Chloe followed her to the edge of the field where there was enough shade to drop the temperature by a stingy three or four degrees. Even that small bit of relief felt welcome.

Chloe chugged a bottle of water that tasted like more, so she popped the top on another.

"I finally got access to the tip line yesterday. There were some pretty bizarre comments on there."

"You've been holding out on me. Dish." EV ordered.

"Most of it was obvious fantasy. Someone actually had an elaborate theory that aliens had taken Luther up in their spaceship, and when they were returning him, something went wrong and he fell to his death." Skepticism and a healthy dose of derision raised Chloe's eyebrows. "Oh, and there were no fewer than four calls from people who thought the 'weird sisters' cast a spell."

"None of that surprises me. The alien one was probably Sabra; she's obsessed with aliens."

160

"Well, there's one that might be useful—someone saw Ashton Worth hanging around the church on the night Luther died. When you add that to his being the one who perpetuated the most gossip about you killing Evan, it's certainly suspicious."

"Ooh, that's interesting," EV speculated. "Any idea who left the tip?"

"Woman's voice—stage whisper, hard to tell—but she used the term 'catting around' which isn't something you hear too often these days."

After a moment of staring into space with a thoughtful expression, EV said, "I can't picture mild little Ashton having the stones to kill anyone. Or the motive for it, come to that. As far as I know, he hasn't had any work done by Luther at his place recently," she ticked off possibilities. "And I don't ever remember seeing he and Evan together."

"Maybe he has a thing for Talia and got rid of Luther so he could..." Chloe broke off as the mental image of Ashton and Talia assaulted her mind. "And now I'm picturing it. Quick, say something to make it go away."

"Aren't you the one who was convinced Evan was bouncing on Talia? She must be quite the *femme fatale* under that fluffy exterior."

"Who else has a motive?"

"Lottie for one."

"Wait, I've heard this all before: how Lottie thought Talia married beneath her, and was jealous that her younger sister found a husband first."

"No, there's more to the story. When Talia started dating Luther, Lottie was off in Warren going to college for a degree in hospitality management or some such. Talia worked for an insurance company in Gilmore and lived at home. I guess the plan was for Talia to save up enough to build or buy a place, and then she and Lottie would run it together. "

"How on earth do you find out all this stuff?"

"Talia applied for a grant through the co-op program."

"Ah, okay." Chloe gestured for her to continue on. The longer they talked, the less time she would have to spend in sweaty labor.

"I'm not quite clear on how Talia and Luther came to start dating, but once they did, all hell broke loose between her and Lottie. Talia decided she would rather get married than go into the B&B business, and when Lottie found out they had an epic battle in the middle of one of the festivals. I can't remember which one. Talia and Luther eloped the next night. Lottie never forgave her for that."

"So how did Lottie end up with the B&B, then?"

"Talia followed through on the grant, put up the difference from her own savings, and presented the whole thing to Lottie as a gift. You'd think that would have brought the two of them together, but it drove them even farther apart. Lottie accused Talia of trying to buy her off; Talia accused Lottie of trying to run her life. They've been fighting off and on ever since. More on than off, really."

"Interesting, but it still only gives Lottie motive for Luther if she thinks getting him out the way would put her ambitions back on track."

"Unless she knew something we don't about Evan's plans once he pushed through the annexation and became mayor." EV was reaching with that one and she knew it.

"Doesn't track for me but I guess we shouldn't rule it out. It's the best theory we have right now. Maybe we can run some of this by Talia tomorrow when we help her with the thank you notes for Luther and Evan's funerals." Butter wouldn't melt in Chloe's mouth as she dropped this particular bomb on EV.

"We're doing what, now? I think I'd remember agreeing to take on something like that." EV's withering glare didn't phase Chloe in the least.

"I ran into Talia yesterday and she kept talking about not being able to face the task. And, I remembered how you thought we should confront her. Before I knew it, I'd volunteered us to help."

"You were the one who thought we should confront her; I said leave it alone. And just when were you planning to tell me?"

"Right now. Break's over." Cucumber picking was starting to look like the lesser of two evils compared to listening to an EV tirade about being shanghaied into doing something she would rather not do.

"Payback will be swift and uncompromising," was EV's parting shot.

"Yeah, yeah. Whatever." Chloe grinned.

Chapter 26

Talia greeted her helpers with a hug and a huge mug of coffee, which EV figured she would probably need in order to get the job done. She'd rather be picking squash bugs in the fields. It was all Chloe's fault for accepting this chore, and EV intended to make her pay for it. A nice blind date ought to do it.

She took a gulp, then nearly choked on the flavor of whiskey. A second, more cautious, sip revealed there was just enough coffee in it to give the whiskey flavor, and not the other way around. It had just gone noon; so a little earlier than EV normally drank alcohol. But then again, this was exactly the type of chore that might require some blurring around the edges. Still, when she set her cup down on the table, it was with the intent not to pick it up again.

From what she could see, Talia probably wouldn't be winning any awards for her organizational skills: sympathy cards spread across the table like they'd been tossed there without thought. Meanwhile, the normally quiet Talia was talking a mile a minute.

"...I put Mrs. Peeves in the kitchen, but then little Austin cried and cried, so I had to let her out."

EV nodded absently, letting Chloe field the conversation while taking a moment to look around. She assumed both Mrs.

Peeves and little Austin were cats, since the room seemed ripe with them. Talia lived in one of the oldest homes in Ponderosa Pines; it was hard to tell, though, since Luther had remodeled parts of the interior to disguise all evidence of energy efficient building. Sheetrock camouflaged the log ends in the living room half of the open floor plan living-dining combo, and also covered up the spectacular bottle-end window Luther's father had worked into the front wall. He would have liked to do more, but the board turned down his request for special dispensation for violating the require percentage of recycled materials.

The kitchen was closed off from the other two main rooms by an old swinging door, with a porthole window that probably came from a fifties-era diner. Presumably, it had been too heavy for Mrs. Peeves to manage.

From where he crouched on the stairs, one yellow tiger cat eyed EV with curiosity, and she could feel more eyes than just his on her: there were cats *everywhere*. One pair belonged to the fattest white feline she had ever seen; his girth sprawled over a brightly patterned afghan thrown across a pale blue, overstuffed chair. Judging by the way his bugged-out bright green eyes darted around the room, EV sensed that he wanted nothing more than to run and hide, but his inherent laziness kept him firmly in place.

In matching powder blue, the longest leg of an L-shaped sectional sofa divided the dining area from the living room, and faced a massive, open-hearth fireplace set with decorative fieldstone. Regardless of his affinity for duping customers and trying to skate around regulations, Luther had been skilled with mortar and stone. He had set several niches into the wide chimney face to serve as shelves. A couple of these had been taken over by lounging felines.

Really? Talia had never given off the crazy cat lady vibe.

Curiosity finally forced the question from EV, "Which one is Mrs. Peeves?"

Talia pointed to the enormous white cat. "Lottie dropped her off here the night Luther died."

166

When Talia excused herself to top off her own coffee mug, both Chloe and EV refused a refill. As soon as Talia left the room, they exchanged astonished expressions.

"Did you see…" Chloe whispered as she waved in the general direction of the cat menagerie.

Nodding, EV whispered back, "Uh, yeah. And the coffee? That stuff would strip the paint off a battleship."

"I know. It's…shh, here she comes."

A pair of Siamese kittens pranced through the kitchen door before it swung shut, upping the total in the room to at least eight. The fatter of the two made a beeline for Chloe, climbed her leg like it was a tree, and then settled into her lap. Contented purring filled the air. Enchanted, she stroked the downy, soft fur of his head while the second little ball of fur went berserk. For no apparent reason, she hopped straight up in the air to land with arched back and tail fluffed out like a bottle brush, then skittered across the floor and disappeared under the couch.

Mere seconds passed before she was back, racing around the room like a miniature tornado. The burst of fury continued as the kitten made a spectacular leap from the back of the sofa to the edge of the table where the three women sat, then scampered across its surface knocking several envelopes to the floor.

At this point, Talia made a half-hearted attempt to catch the tawny ball of energy before it could inflict any more damage.

"Come here, Mummy's little snuggy wuggums," Talia cooed to the kitten, who took great offense to the baby talk and renewed her efforts to wreak havoc. When Talia dodged left, the kitten banked right, launched herself off the sofa back to slide across the surface of a nearby console table and send its contents crashing to the floor. That nothing on the table had been breakable was evidence this was not her first time playing the trick.

More baby talk seemed to further enrage the kitten.

"Who's a cute little sugar baby? Come to Mummy, sweetie."

It was EV who ended the chase when the kitten swerved around Talia, then leapt onto the table. As the tiny terrorist skated across the table, scattering the envelopes Chloe had once again neatened into a pile, EV's hand shot out and snatched the little beast on her way past.

Cradling the blue-eyed cutie in her hands, EV held the kitten at eye level and gave her a much needed lecture on proper cat behavior. Instead of appearing chastened, Mummy's little *snuggy wuggums* reached out a claw-sheathed paw to touch EV's nose in reverence. Her purr filled the air.

"What's her name?"

Talia quirked an eyebrow, "After that performance, I'm thinking her name should be *Thing One* or *Thing Two* but I've been calling her *Sugar*." She pointed to the kitten in Chloe's lap, "And that one is *Spice*. Horis found the pair of them in his barn, covered with fleas and hungry. He asked me to foster them while he tried to find good homes. We treated the fleas and got them their shots, but I swear, Sugar hates me. I hope we can find a place for them, but it seems a shame to break them up when they've been through so much already." Talia's voice turned husky with the sympathy for the kittens. It seemed obvious to Chloe and EV that Talia was projecting her own feelings onto them.

A blind date and a pair of furry new roommates, EV's revenge would take more than one form.

Chloe changed the subject back to the reason for this visit.

"What can we do to help you with these Thank You notes, Talia?"

It might have been the two cups—at least—of the Irish coffee Talia had consumed, but when she answered, her voice sounded as quivery as an elderly auntie's. "I wish Lottie and I could find a way to bury the hatchet; she should be the one helping me right now."

When she felt Chloe's foot nudge hers under the table, EV decided to take charge of the job at hand, and gently moved little Sugar to a spot on the back of the couch before gathering up all of the condolence cards strewn across the table. The funeral home had provided a list of floral tributes along with more unopened cards.

"I'll address the envelopes." Chloe volunteered, having seen plenty of EV's lousy penmanship.

"Talia," EV spoke in a soothing voice, "under the circumstances, I think everyone will understand if you combine your notes for Luther and Evan.". Within a few minutes, they had a working system. EV opened the cards, then handed the envelopes off to Chloe to copy the address. Talia penned a sentence or two of thanks before both card and envelope circled back to EV, who stuffed and stamped them. In this manner, they moved along fairly quickly.

While they worked, Chloe started up a conversation with Talia.

"Was there anyone special in Evan's life?"

"I don't think so. He never talked to me about his lady friends, and I never liked to ask. Evan was a private man. He wasn't interested in settling down." There was none of the regret in her voice that might come from having been spurned, which put the final death knell to the theory she had ever been the object of Evan's affection.

They were nearing the end of the pile when EV frowned. There was something about the handwriting on this card that reminded her of something she had seen recently.

Then it hit her.

She had seen that *S* before.

Trying not to give away anything with her facial expression, EV read out the card, then when she handed it to Chloe, delivered a swift but gentle kick to the ankle along with it. EV ignored Chloe's dirty look and used exaggerated eye and head movements to get Chloe to look at the handwriting without alerting Talia that anything was wrong.

As Chloe realized what she was looking at, her mouth dropped open, and they both noted the signature on the card. Unless there were two people with that distinctive style, the person who signed this card was the one who had been threatening Luther.

Chapter 27

Why do I let that crazy old bat talk me into these things? Was the main question on Chloe's mind as two rambunctious kittens zig-zagged across the floor of her formerly pristine living room. At EV's suggestion—and she used the term extremely loosely—the kittens had been packed up and delivered to her door early this morning. After being released from the prison of their shiny new cat carrier, Sugar and Spice made a beeline for the fireplace mantle, where they systematically knocked over several items of kitsch belonging to Chloe's mother.

By way of a semi-acrobatic back bend, Chloe managed to catch all but a tiny cat figurine, which she had never really cared for anyway. A cat for two kittens seemed like a good trade off, and as she swept the pieces into the dustbin, Chloe began looking around the room for other items that might need to be moved to accommodate her new pets. Spice was currently guarding a spot in the center of the mantle, while keeping an eye on his sister who was alternately sniffing and rubbing against a nubby chenille throw draped across the back of an oversize armchair.

Hearing some noise undetectable to Chloe, four ears perked and both kittens raced through the open porch door and launched themselves onto a window screen, legs splayed in all directions. Gently detaching their claws Chloe admonished them ruefully.

"No, no, these are not climbing posts. You stay down." They both looked at her, cocked their heads to one side and marched back to the living room. "Good kitties," Chloe murmured, hoping without much confidence that they would continue to listen this well. She had a feeling she'd need to do less baby-proofing if she had an actual baby.

The vast array of kitten paraphernalia littering Chloe's floor was similar to the amount of unnecessary accessories often purchased by new mothers. Several catnip-filled mice were already strewn around the living room; a scratching post that would most likely be discarded in favor of an arm of the couch was propped up near the fireplace; and a plastic stick with feathers attached poked out from beneath an end table. Several varieties of cat food, new bowls, and a self-cleaning kitty litter setup were already at home in Chloe's kitchen and bathroom. As EV had predicted, the two former orphans would certainly be well taken care of.

Chloe gathered her tablet and snuggled into her favorite porch chair to sort through the notes she and EV had made regarding Evan and Luther's murders. Sugar and Spice nestled themselves in the crevices between her thighs and the arms of the chair, one on each side, and fell asleep purring. Now it was time to get down to brass tacks.

She began compiling a list of evidence for and against their two prime suspects, Lottie and Ashton Worth. Lottie had several marks against her, after frequently and publicly declaring her dislike for both Evan and Luther.

The way Chloe saw it, Lottie could be guilty of the murders, but not the blackmail. It would explain why she acted so strangely around Talia lately, and why she had gone mysteriously quiet regarding the whole business. It wasn't like Lottie to keep her mouth shut, so she must have a good reason for doing so.

The only thing that didn't gel was why she would have told Chloe and EV about Evan being blackmailed in the first place. Come to think of it, neither method of murder screamed Lottie; Chloe had a feeling she'd choose something more eloquent than a push off a ladder or a bashed in skull. Then again, if the murders weren't planned it could have been a crime of passion or opportunity, and the killer would have used any means necessary.

With Ashton, it was the other way around. His name now had two marks against it: he was undoubtedly the person who wrote the threatening note to Luther; his handwriting on the condolence card was a slam dunk. And, he was seen at the scene of the crime, very close to the time of Luther's death. But what could possibly be his motive for either murder, or for his newfound hatred of EV?

Ashton writing the blackmail letter to Luther seemed to clinch the idea that he had also killed him; if Lottie also knew Ashton wrote the notes she may have used that as more ammo to frame him. Each theory seemed to circle back to the other suspect. Frustrated, she put her tablet away and moved to get up. Tiny claws dug through her shorts and into her skin; apparently her furry friends weren't ready to end their snuggle session. Luckily, a merciful and well-timed knock on the door was too much for them to ignore, so Chloe got her way and rose from the chair.

Chapter 28

Spice leapt into the air, his lithe body nearly twisting and turning as he pounced on a crumpled piece of paper. He snatched it up in his mouth and leapt again, a shake of his head sending the toy into EV's lap. She picked it up with the idea of tossing it back to him, when she realized it was a receipt from Thread. Priscilla used bright purple ink in her register, making the receipts easy to distinguish at a glance.

With an arch look at Chloe, she started to unfold it, then had to dodge to the right as Chloe tried to grab it away from her. After a brief but fierce tussle, EV got to sneak a peek.

"Yarn?"

"It's not for me, I was buying it for a friend." If her words had not been accompanied by a guilty look, EV might have bought it, but outside of not confessing her role as town gossip columnist, Chloe was a lousy liar. She only held out a minute before confessing, "Fine. I thought I'd learn how to knit. Everyone says it's relaxing."

"Not the way I do it," EV grumbled. "You might as well come to knitting group with me and let Priscilla show you the basics."

"I can just watch a YouTube video."

"And will a YouTube video tell you if you're using too much tension when you wrap the yarn?"

"No," Chloe groaned.

"You'll come with me and learn properly. Consider it your punishment for keeping secrets."

"Knitting group is a punishment? Why, what goes on there? Some kind of old lady confessional where you all talk about support hose and why things aren't like they were in the 'good old days', I'll bet."

"You're going, Miss Recluse."

"Fine, I'll go." At this point, there was little other choice. EV was like a dog with a bone when she used that tone of voice. Besides, Chloe couldn't deny the term struck a nerve; she had promised herself that she would be more outgoing, but so far had not made good.

As much as she told herself she belonged in Ponderosa Pines—and even though she was accepted almost without question—Chloe still couldn't see herself as a true member of the community; as actually having found the place where she belonged. With an evil glance back at EV, she added, "But I'm driving."

Now it was EV's turn to groan. "We can walk."

"It's raining."

"Not that hard." Rain pelted the window. "Besides, it's supposed to clear off by noon."

"Hard enough." EV went back for her knitting bag before settling into place in the passenger seat. She had barely gotten her seat belt locked when Chloe threw the car into gear and rocketed down the drive.

The first face they saw as they stepped through the door was Lottie's.

"One of us should try to talk to her; see if we can get her to reconcile with Talia." EV kept her voice low enough that only Chloe could hear.

"Not it." Chloe's declaration was met with a pair of eloquently raised eyebrows.

"Not it? Really? How mature."

"You dragged me here, you can talk to dragon lady." Chloe chose a seat near Priscilla.

There were plenty to spare, since besides Lottie and Allegra, only two other knitters had braved the rain. EV settled onto the sofa and pulled out her knitting bag.

Clearly, the textile genius had not been passed down from mother to daughter, because the mess that stretched between EV's two needles resembled nothing like the dishcloth it was supposed to be.

A simple square in heavy cotton shouldn't be that hard to produce, but it was beyond EV's capabilities to create anything better than a misshapen tangle of knots that only loosely qualified as knitting.

As expected, though, after a short demonstration, Chloe was producing lovely, even rows at a speed that rivaled Priscilla's. EV shot her the stink eye while Chloe returned a smirk.

"Lottie, how are you and Talia getting along?" Looking down at her work while trying to untangle the yarn that had somehow tied itself around her finger, EV missed seeing the anguished look that came over Lottie's face. Chloe caught it along with the trembling of Lottie's bottom lip. The woman was close to tears. Had Lofty Lottie finally been taken down by her formally mousy sister? It looked like it.

"She won't speak to me. I've tried to apologize, but she won't listen. She won't even look at me," Lottie's voice held genuine regret as she slumped down in her seat, defeated.

"Give her some time," Allegra advised. "Talia's had a lot to handle these past few weeks, and frankly, you didn't do much to help." Her tone was gentle but the rebuke was clear.

"I know. I want to make it up to her, but she won't let me."

Allegra shrugged. Given her performance at both Luther and Evan's funerals, everyone knew Lottie had a long way to go before Talia would even consider forgiveness.

While Chloe focused on Lottie, EV gave up all pretense of knitting to study Allegra's face and posture. At the last knitting group, she had been completely scattered and inattentive; today, she appeared more calm but there was also sadness underneath the facade and EV could see tension. It was there in the set of her mouth; the pinched look around her eyes—yet, her needles clicked together in perfect rhythm while her hands moved smoothly through the motions of knitting.

"Maybe if you had been more considerate of her feelings, she wouldn't be shutting you out this way. She lost her husband, and for a few days, it looked like he might have died by his own brother's hand. Then Evan died, and the police don't have any idea who killed either of them. I've been a nervous wreck for days." Allegra didn't notice her slip of the tongue, but EV and Chloe both picked up on it right away.

A look passed between them, but with a barely perceptible shake of her head, EV communicated to Chloe that now was not the time to pursue that line of questioning.

"What's worse is that someone started a rumor that she was having an affair with Evan." Allegra's eyes sparked as though she had a personal stake in the situation.

"That's ridiculous. I know for a fact *she* was not the one Evan was sleeping with," Lottie tossed her head, and though the accusation in her tone was not directed at anyone in particular it was clear someone in the room was meant to feel the sting of her barb.

"It's almost as ludicrous as thinking EV killed him, but we all know how that rumor got tossed around so much." Priscilla glanced at Allegra, whose face reddened.

Allegra opened her mouth, presumably to defend her husband, then closed it again.

"Well, I hope people don't put too much credence in the word of a man who goes out catting around."

On hearing the remark, both Chloe and EV's hands stilled, and a look passed between them. Lottie had no idea that her chance remark would be caught by the two people in town who had already heard her use nearly the same phrase and inflection before. There was no doubt, Lottie was the tipster.

Could she be both the tipster and the murderer?

Seated next to her, Chloe noticed Allegra's hands were shaking, and a sideways glance at her face proved that she had turned pale. EV noticed the same thing, watching with interest as Allegra dropped one stitch, then another.

For several minutes, there was no other sound, save for the clacking of needles.

Just as Chloe cleared her throat to say something—anything—that might reduce the tension, Allegra abruptly thrust her knitting back into her bag and announced with fake brightness, "Ladies, I believe I'll just nip out a little early this week."

Her remark was met with only half-hearted protest.

As Allegra made ready to leave, she pulled a colorful scarf from her bag and, turning away from the group, began to wrap it over her hair. Behind her, Chloe's face took on an astonished expression—mouth dropping to her chin; eyebrows shooting up nearly to her hairline. She waved a hand to get EV's attention.

"Scarf!" she mouthed and pointed.

That was the moment everything fell into place.

Chapter 29

Steam rolled off the sidewalk under the shimmering rays of the sun where it peeked through the lightening cloud cover. The Mudbucket's eaves dripped and dribbled their watery burden onto the pavement below. The water ran and puddled as Chloe and EV hurried in to snag EV's favorite table; the one near the kitchen door.

This was a conversation too distracting to have while driving.

"Evan and Allegra?" EV kept her voice low. "She's the cougar Lottie was talking about. Can't say I was expecting that."

"I know, right? We know Ashton wrote the note to Luther, and he was at the church, and he had a motive for killing Evan." Chloe ticked each point off on her fingers. "He's the one, you know he did it."

"It all fits."

"Filthy bastard tried to implicate you. That's why he started all those rumors."

"There's one thing I still can't wrap my head around, though. What was the motive for killing Luther? Lottie had more reason to want him dead than Ashton."

"You think they were in it together? Maybe Lottie killed Luther and Ashton wasted Evan?"

"No," EV mused, "If she was in on it, the last thing she would do is call the tip line. She defended me whenever she heard someone repeating stupid gossip. It had to be Ashton all the way."

"What if Luther knew and threatened to go public with the affair? Ashton might have killed him to save face." Chloe dumped extra sugar into her coffee.

"I guess...it still seems off to me. The real question is: what do we do now?"

Chloe tapped her fingers on the table. The smart thing to do would be to call Nate and lay it out for him, but she wanted one more chance to settle it all in her mind.

"We don't have to decide now; let's go back to your place, look at the time lines, and see if everything fits before we go accusing someone with no hard evidence."

After the tingle that had run through her, EV knew they were on the right track, but it never hurt to be thorough. She reached for her knitting bag but came up empty-handed.

"I think I left my bag at Thread, I'll just grab it and then we can go."

***

Ashton stepped out from where he had been standing in the hallway that led to the kitchen and restrooms. The shadowy corner made a perfect cover as he exited the men's room and heard his name mentioned. Now, his face an unreadable mask, he walked out of the Mudbucket and right past his wife, who stood in the recessed doorway of New Sage, a shopping bag in each hand.

***

Allegra watched, dumbfounded, as her husband cast a furtive glance toward Thread, hurried to their car, pulled a gun out of the glove box, and drove away toward the side of town where EV lived.

Something was terribly wrong.

When EV and Chloe walked out of Thread, then drove away in the same direction, she was sure of it.

Where had Ashton gotten that gun. For that matter, *when* had Ashton gotten that gun.

Allegra dropped both shopping bags before fumbling in her purse for her cell phone. She placed a hurried call to Nate to warn him that he needed to get to EV's, and fast. It was a gamble whether the others were headed there, but there was little time to waste on indecision so she went with intuition.

Since Ashton had taken the car and she had stood there like an idiot while Chloe drove away, Allegra needed another way to get to EV's place, but there was no other vehicle in sight. Just her luck.

Where were all the nosy neighbors when she really needed one?

It had been a long time, years, since Allegra had run full out. Probably since high school. But she had lettered in track—middle distance and 100 meter sprints—and even if she had let herself go a bit, she knew she had at least one good effort left in her.

Three steps in stiletto heels was far enough to prove she would never make it in time so Allegra kicked them off, tossed her purse and bags under the display table outside of New Sage, and rummaged around in a bin full of hot pink canvas mules for a pair that fit. A pang of guilt over shoplifting fluttered through her mind, but right now she had more important things to worry about.

Allegra slipped the shoes on and ran like the hounds of hell were on her heels: across the street, down toward the church, and into the woods.

183

She took EV's shortcut, lengthening her stride to eat up the distance as fast as her feet would carry her. Cutting across country this way was not quite as quick as driving, but because the road to that side of town was a series of switchbacks, Ashton would have to go slow. It would be close.

***

Twice on the way to EV's house, distraction and speed nearly cost Ashton precious control of his car on a curve, but he pulled it out at the last minute. *Confession is good for the soul*—it was the one clear thought running through his mind while he hid his vehicle in the trees at the end of the cul-de-sac. When he was sure it couldn't be seen, Ashton doubled back to test EV's back door. It was open—almost no one locked their doors in Ponderosa Pines.

Because nothing bad ever happened here. Until now.

When he saw the crime scene photos spread across her dining room, Luther's staring eyes sent a shudder through him; but it was the garish puddle of red spreading out from under Evan's head that had Ashton riveted. The stark images turned his stomach.

He'd done that.

To another human being.

The gun hung forgotten at his side while tears ran down his face. He stood like a statue even when Chloe preceded EV through the front door.

***

Barely inside the room, Chloe caught sight of Ashton and quickly noticed the gun in his hand. Her knees turned to jelly; her heart kicked into a gallop; and her feet refused to carry her another inch.

"What the…" The words died in EV's mouth when a wide-eyed Chloe leaned to the side so EV could see, and pointed to the man who shouldn't have been there.

"Holy sh—" Chloe elbowed EV hard in the ribs and mouthed, "Do something!"

"Ow," EV muttered absently; her brain busy running through various scenarios. Finally, she asked the question that seemed most logical: "What are you doing here, Ashton?"

"I didn't mean to do it."

"Of course not." EV fought to keep her voice calm and soothing.

"We know Evan and Allegra were sleeping together, but why Luther? What did he do?" Chloe gave in to curiosity. Who knew what might happen in the next few minutes; she could at least die without that question on her mind. If they could keep him talking, some miracle might bring help.

Before he could explain exactly what Luther had done, Allegra burst through the door shouting, "I think Ashton killed Luther and Evan, and is on his way here! He has a gun!"

Not a miracle.

EV waved a hand with exaggerated impatience to show Allegra she was too late.

"Hello, Allegra." Ashton's face reddened; his voice turned cold. "Why don't you come see what I did to your lover."

The situation had just gone from bad to worse in the space of a heartbeat.

Chloe edged closer toward the kitchen island, thinking it might provide some protection if the gun went off. She dragged EV with her, inch by slow inch, while Ashton preoccupied himself with his wife.

Allegra swallowed hard but refused to look at the copies of the crime scene photos. Instead, she focused all of her attention on Ashton.

"It meant nothing."

"Don't lie to me again." Ashton's voice rose.

Chloe drove her elbow into EV's ribs for the second time. "Do something, now!"

"Ashton," her tone the same she would use on a child who needed to calm down, "why don't you tell us what happened," EV urged. "You'll feel better if you get it off your chest."

Catching Allegra's eye, she tried to communicate to the woman that being quiet was in her best interest.

"Start with what happened to Luther so we can understand, and help you."

The next minute felt an eternity long. The tension in the room was palpable while Ashton considered her request. Finally, he nodded twice and began to speak.

Chapter 30

"It all started the night of the town meeting. Allegra and I have been…well, we haven't been communicating on a deeper level for a few months now, if you know what I mean." As sexual innuendo goes, this was probably the mildest one ever, but it fit perfectly with Ashton's normal speech patterns. Always proper—even pedantic at times—but with a touch of drama.

He waited until both EV and Chloe nodded their understanding before continuing.

"My mind was a whirlwind of conflicting thoughts as I watched the two of them over the course of the evening. Until that night, I hoped I had been mistaken; that I had taken the admiring looks between Evan and Allegra for something more than what they were: the innocent glances between two people who agree on an issue. My wife is an attractive woman, and I could never blame a man for thinking so. But as the night wore on, unless it was my imagination, Allegra's eyes seemed to seek Evan out with a hunger that she should be keeping only for me, her husband.

Still, I couldn't accuse her without evidence, so I watched and waited a few days until one night, when she fell asleep before me.

I'm not as stupid as people think. It only took me a few minutes to crack the password on her cell phone—*password* is not a safe password, Allegra—and there it was, in black and white. Texts, emails, phone logs: proof.

Did she think she could pull the wool over my eyes forever? No, it was time to face facts; my wife was having an affair with the sleaziest scumbag in town.

Anger, in a pulsing wave of emotion, rose up to swamp me; its red fire sending my blood pressure soaring, tightening my collar until it felt like I might choke on the emotion. I had to get out of there; my feet carried me on an aimless path that eventually led me down Winding Road Lane.

I stood in the warm wash of a street lamp with fists clenched, until my nails dug bloody crescents in the flesh of my palms.

No. I forced the anger back to fold in on itself like a newly-washed shirt. Allegra loved me. She might cheat, but she would never leave me. Beat by beat, my heart rate slowed; my mind cleared to a dead calm. No. Everything was fine. A good marriage involved forgiveness. I had to remember that.

Finally calm, I turned back. Preoccupation with my thoughts had carried me a long way from home. When I heard voices coming from the church, I promise you I intended to turn away, but a name caught my attention. Without thinking twice, I slid into the shadows between a yew bush and the wall near the window, being careful to keep my steps silent, and listened.

What I heard turned my blood cold, then hot again, and stunned me so thoroughly that when one of the conversationalists departed the church to stroll past where I stood hidden from sight, I never even moved.

I was still standing there, minutes later when a white cat streaked past me to leap through the window. I could hear Luther whistling while he worked. I heard him yell at the cat; the next thing I heard was a muted cry followed by a thump. I was still standing there while Luther died."

Ashton turned toward the women so they could see the tears of anguish forming.

"You have to believe me, I had no idea what happened. If I had known, I would have tried to help. I swear I would have. No matter what you might think of me, I didn't kill Luther. It wasn't murder; it was some kind of accident. The cat must have slammed into the ladder. You know how rickety it was, everyone who's used it knows that."

Gently, since she was in a position to know the facts, EV assured him, "There was nothing you could have done for Luther. Nothing anyone could have done."

Her words had no effect; Ashton waved the gun around while the three women huddled together. Allegra had joined EV and Chloe behind the island.

Seeming unable to speak, Allegra bowed her head in shame. Every so often, she shook with silent tears.

"I had no beef with Luther. It wasn't his fault his brother couldn't keep his hands to himself. I never wanted Luther dead. But when everyone thought he was murdered, it gave me ideas. I'm a lot smarter than people think I am," he repeated.

"You hear that, Allegra? I'm not an idiot. You're the stupid one. He joked about it. Did you know that? You were nothing but a joke. He laughed about dancing in the sheets with someone else's wife. I heard him telling Luther about the blackmail notes, and figured I could use the situation to my advantage."

Tears clogged Ashton's voice. "He was holding one of the notes when he...when I hit him. After it was all over, I took it and used it to forge one for Luther. Then I dropped it in the box at Evan's funeral. I figured if everyone thought the blackmailer killed them both, I'd be off the hook. All I meant to do was scare him into staying away from my wife, but then I heard them talking on the phone and my brain just clicked off. Everything went red and then...then Evan was dead.'"

Chloe caught EV's eye; this was the answer to why an empty envelope was among the items found at the scene of the crime.

"How did you get into his house?" Chloe tried to distract him, to buy more time. Maybe he would calm down enough to put the gun down before anyone got hurt, or worse, killed.

"This is Ponderosa Pines; nothing bad ever happens here. He left his doors unlocked just like everybody else does. There he was, so busy celebrating over fighting with EV, and then breaking my wife's heart, he didn't hear me when I walked up behind him. But I could hear you, Allegra, crying and begging him for one more chance to be together."

"Let me get this straight," EV's words fell like desert dust, "You killed him—not just because he was sleeping with your wife—but because he broke up with her and made her cry?"

The man was batcrap crazy with a side of loose screws.

Chapter 31

When the call came in from Allegra, Nate had been in the unenviable position of standing between two invective-spitting sisters. Talia Plunkett and Lottie Calabrese were either going to make up or kill each other, and at this point, Nate wasn't sure which one he preferred.

Having been raised by peace-loving parents who instilled them with a sense of propriety, the two women broke off the argument long enough to let him answer the phone.

"Hello."

"Ashton's headed toward EV Torrence's place and he's got a gun."

"Allegra?"

"I'm going after him. Chloe and EV are on their way home. Hurry," she hung up.

Nate turned to Talia, "you two are going to have to work this out without me." He punched speed dial on his phone, "I need backup at EV Torrence's place; Ashton Worth is over there and he's looking for trouble. Watch yourself, Burnsoll, he's armed." Nate's uniformed butt barely touched his car seat before

191

Talia and Lottie, fight forgotten, made a beeline for Lottie's *Prius*.

***

Struggling to keep her tone quiet and even while every nerve in her body vibrated, Chloe filled the silence, "Ashton, Allegra's crying can't you hear her? She frightened and needs you to console her. Don't you, Allegra?"

When Allegra continued to shudder, Chloe gave her the elbow, and followed it up with a tiny shove. Getting in between a homicidal maniac and his emotional trigger was just about the last thing she wanted to do today, and she silently cursed herself for not calling Nate the minute she and EV knew Ashton was the killer. If pushing Allegra into the fray was what it took to stay alive, she was all in with that.

"No. No. No. She doesn't need me, that's clearer than ever, now." Ashton's voice quavered. "There's only one thing left to do."

"But she does need you. Look at her, Ashton. Look at her." He turned his head away.

"Talk to him, Allegra. Right now," Chloe hissed at the woman. "Before he kills us all. This is your mess; now you clean it up."

When Allegra finally opened her mouth, what came out was completely unexpected, "Shoot me, Ashton. Please just kill me. I can't bear to live knowing all the pain I've caused." Allegra stumbled away from the scant protection provided by the kitchen island, taking several tentative steps toward her husband.

"No. Don't come any closer," he all but shrieked at her. The gun rose upward to slam, barrel first, into his temple. His finger slid onto the trigger.

"Stop!" Allegra cried out. "Don't, please Ashton, please. For me."

192

"Why? You don't want me, haven't wanted me for a long time. I've killed someone, Allegra. There's no coming back from this. I've lost everything. Everything. Don't come any closer."

Ashton's finger twitched, began to squeeze, but Allegra kept walking.

Chloe dropped to the floor, grabbed EV's arm, and dragged her down, out of the line of fire.

The next thing they heard was the crash of breaking glass as Nate burst through the window and slammed into Ashton, knocking the gun free from his hands. Dalton used the door, but it was all over before he cleared the frame.

All the fight gone out of him, Ashton sobbed while Nate secured his hands behind his back, and left him to lie among glittering shards of window glass before rounding the island to see for himself whether Chloe was hurt. His words were terse, his voice strained, when he ordered Dalton: "See to Allegra."

He pulled first EV then Chloe to their feet, and checked them for damage before giving Chloe a shake. "What were you thinking? You don't chase after criminals; you could have been hurt."

"Technically, he chased after us," Chloe tried to pull Nate's hands away, but he held her firmly and enveloped her into a tight hug. A chill that had nothing to do with recently being cornered by a madman with a gun ran up her spine. Chloe pressed her head to Nate's chest, felt his heart racing in rhythm with her own. "I'm fine," she said softly, looking up into the ocean blue of his eyes. "Nice tackle, by the way."

"Are you sure you're not hurt?" he asked, concern still coloring his face. "If anything had happened to you…" He pulled her close again before giving her another shake. "Chloe, you know you're the one…"

"You're the one who's bleeding, Nathaniel." EV gently pointed out before reaching for the first aid kit she kept in one of her kitchen drawers. Chloe could have killed her for interrupting at that particular moment. Nate had been about to say something

193

interesting. Half a dozen shallow nicks testified to Nate's trip through the window. With whatever moment they had been about to have now passed, Chloe cleaned and treated each one with gentle hands, while EV turned her own attention to Allegra.

A small gash on Allegra's cheek dripped a stream of red, but EV was more concerned for the woman's emotional state. Her shaking hands felt chilled; her face so pale that the drops of blood stood out in startling relief. EV gave Dalton's arm a squeeze before pulling Allegra away from him to settle her on the sofa with a crooked afghan. Using her voice as a soothing balm, EV reassured Allegra while she gently cleaned the cut, closed it with a butterfly bandage, then moved on to similarly treat Ashton.

As much trouble as he had caused, Ashton made a pitiful sight with tears and snot running down his face.

A flurry of activity followed Nate's spectacular take-down, making it impossible for he and Chloe to get a moment alone. She was starting to realize that EV might be right; her feelings for Nate were not as firmly planted in the friend zone as she would like to admit. Still, it didn't change the fact that he would hightail it as soon as he could. Regardless, now was not the time to sort out her feelings; people were still milling about, and probably would be for at least another couple of hours.

As if on cue, Talia and Lottie arrived with much skidding and screeching of tires, and stayed long after the State Troopers had taken Ashton off to jail. To her surprise, Chloe was happy to see both of them, and greeted each with an uncharacteristically warm hug.

It turned out that Nate had been standing outside the window recording Ashton's confession, and had only taken action when he threatened to kill himself. Once in police custody, Ashton clammed up. But the standard pat down turned up an envelope with Allegra's name on it, containing a lengthy, tear-splotched confession written in his own hand.

Even as he was being hauled into custody, Ashton maintained he had never intended to harm EV or Chloe. No one was buying it.

Allegra, it was decided, would spend the night in EV's guest room while Nate searched her house for evidence to support Ashton's confession and ensure a conviction. She, along with EV and Chloe, scheduled a meeting with Dalton for the following day to make their official statements.

Before leaving, Dalton turned to EV, "You still owe me a night of dancing. Friday. I'll pick you up at 8:00." Then, before she had time to deflect, he pulled her against him and planted a searing kiss on her lips while Chloe hooted and cheered. Dalton's face was red, but his grin was a mile wide when he turned to leave.

He never saw EV brush a hand over her mouth as she watched him walk away.

If EV thought the withering look she turned on Chloe would have any effect, she was sadly mistaken.

***

Once her heart rate slowed enough to think clearly, curiosity threatened to overwhelm Chloe. Had Allegra suspected Ashton? What did she know? Most of all, how long before Chloe could ask without being considered thoughtless? That elephant was so big it would take up way more than just the one room.

Her eye fell on Lottie. Lottie who had not said a word about being the tipster while Nate was around. Chloe's nose wrinkled at the smell of a good story. First chance she got, she'd pry. Turned out she didn't even have to do that much.

Talia, tearful with relief at learning her Luther had not been murdered, bustled about the kitchen with a broom and dustpan. Everyone noticed, but did not remark on the fact that she continued sweeping long after every piece of glass was gone. Lottie finally grabbed the broom, tossed it away, and pulled her into a fierce hug.

"Oh, Lottie," Talia's voice broke. "I'm sorry for shutting you out."

"Well, you thought it might have been me who killed Luther."

"You knew I suspected you?"

Lottie hugged her again. "It's a sister thing. Luther might not have been my choice for you, but he did his best to make you happy." Left unsaid was anything about his less than ethical business practices.

"It was an accident, not murder," Talia took a deep breath to let the words sink in. "Not murder," she repeated. Relieved of that burden, her spine straightened just a bit. "I've been so worried that whoever killed him might come after me next."

"I never thought...I mean...I have a confession to make." Lottie let go of Talia, and walked to the table where she slumped into a chair and dropped her head in her hands.

After a moment, when she had composed herself, Lottie beckoned Talia to take a seat.

"Please, please don't hate me for this, Tallie, but I was there."

"You...where? I don't understand." Dread bleached the color from Talia's face.

"I was at the church. Not inside, and not when Luther fell."

Chloe shot EV a look, and a swift but gentle kick under the table. The tipster was about to reveal all.

"I finished the book I was reading, but I couldn't find another one in the house that looked interesting, so I decided to walk into town and check the book boxes." Romance novels were Lottie's addiction. "I was just getting ready to turn on my penlight, and check the box across the street from the church when I saw someone sneak into the bushes. It looked suspicious, and I was curious, so I doubled back, crossed the street, and came up on the far side of the rectory."

Her audience sat spellbound, so Lottie continued, "I heard Luther and Evan arguing and plotting. Evan was being blackmailed by someone to push through the Gilmore annexation scheme, and he wanted Luther to help him. I got distracted at first, but when Evan left I remembered the person in the bushes, so I slowly crept to the corner to see if I could tell who it was. The window was open, and there was just enough light that Ashton's face stood out clearly. I figured he was just being nosy, so I turned around and got out of there before he saw me."

"So you were gone before Luther fell? Ashton said a white cat jumped through the window. We'll never know for sure, but we think the cat either jumped onto that rickety ladder, or startled Luther. And that's how he fell."

"Well, I didn't see the cat until I found her crying in the bushes on my way home, but I did see Ashton."

"And you didn't tell anyone? You could have saved Evan if you had spoken up before." Talia's voice rode the edge of bitterness.

"Cut me a break, Tallie, there was no way I could have known what Ashton would do. None of us knew about Allegra. For all I knew, Ashton was the one who was blackmailing Evan."

"No, I guess you couldn't have known," Talia admitted.

"After Evan was killed and Ashton started targeting EV, I called the *Pine Cone* tip line. I didn't know what else to do. By the time I realized he might be connected to Evan's death, you weren't speaking to me, and I was afraid you would think I was meddling. I figured the paper must turn all the tips over to the police, so that was the easiest way to stay anonymous. I thought it was funny, though, that young Nathaniel seemed to talk to everyone but Ashton."

"Tha…" Chloe started to explain until EV delivered a firm kick to her ankle, reminding her no one was supposed to know she had access to the tip line.

197

"…t is strange," she covered quickly then asked, "did you give any details on the tip line?"

Lottie thought it over, "I said I'd seen Ashton near the church on the night Luther died. That's pretty specific, right?"

"Hmm, yeah. Maybe something happened to the line; some kind of technical glitch." Chloe pursed her lips. Time to change the subject before she outed herself.

From where she lay on the couch, a cool cloth over her forehead, Allegra spoke. "I had no idea. I know you all are wondering. Not until knitting group when something Lottie said made it all click into place. Then everything happened so fast. I called Nate, and then ran all the way here to see if I could help, but all I did was fall apart. I could have gotten you all killed. Everything that happened—it's all my fault."

"Don't be ridiculous." EV injected just the right amount of scorn to push her point home. "Husbands get cheated on all the time and don't kill anyone over it. You can't take credit for Ashton's choices; you can only decide to be responsible for your own.

Chapter 32

"All in favor?"

A chorus of *ayes* sounded across the room as the First Selectman called for the vote that put any further discussion of Ponderosa Pines becoming part of Gilmore to rest.

"All opposed?"

All eyes turned toward the fidgeting, bespectacled young man standing in the back of the room before turning toward Allegra Worth. The representative from Gilmore had absolutely no influence in Ponderosa Pines town business; wagers for how long Allegra planned to stick around were the current game of choice, but not a single nay was heard.

"Motion carries." The gavel fell with a ringing sound.

In what Chloe declared an epically stupid decision, EV had chosen not to attend this particular town meeting. Whether her absence communicated her faith that the town would choose the right path, or that she no longer cared what happened made no difference. A number of people in this room owed EV and apology, and if they didn't know that, Chloe intended to tell them.

"You all are unbelievable! For weeks you've been persecuting an innocent woman because she was opposed to merging with Gilmore, and now every single one of you has voted the proposal down? EV Torrence has spent the last month trying to make up for

199

something she didn't even do, and she's the one looking out for your best interests. You all should be begging her to forgive you! What would you do if she decided to leave? Who would you all turn to for guidance then?" Chloe spun on her heel and stalked out the door muttering, "Ungrateful, spiteful, disappointments, the lot of you."

Closing the Grange Hall door behind her, Chloe leaned back against it and tried to calm her beating heart. She had never let loose like that at any kind of town gathering: in fact, Chloe was always polite and soft-spoken; never one to make waves. She imagined what the people inside were thinking and saying about her outburst; imagined the dumbfound expressions on her neighbors' faces. *That'll teach them to mess with me and my friends.*

When she looked up, EV was standing across the street, brimming with curiosity. Chloe bounded over and wrapped her arms around her friend. "I love you, you know," she said simply. EV's smile reciprocated the sentiment, and so did the hard squeeze she gave Chloe before nosiness got the best of her.

"So..."

"Well, the rep from Gilmore—Roger something—maintains that his people were promised some kind of monetary benefit if they agreed to merge with us. He didn't say exactly, but he hinted that some big box business is looking to build in the area. He was under the impression that Gilmore wouldn't see any profits if it happened on Ponderosa Pines property. They don't know their asses from a hole in the ground over there, and he seemed to think we were a bunch of idiots just sitting around waiting for them to swoop in and save us. Now the investor has disappeared, and it turns out he was using an alias. Nathaniel's going to look into it."

It didn't pass unnoticed by EV that Chloe's tone softened when she spoke Nate's name, but she let it go without comment. "Sounds like someone was playing them and Evan at the same time. I'd say we've found—and then lost again—our blackmailer."

"Like I said, Nate's on it."

"So you *don't* want to look into it?" EV smirked, she already knew the answer.

"Research mode?" Chloe's wheels were already spinning with possibilities.

"I'll meet you in your backyard with the peanut butter cups."

***

Several days after her blowup at the town meeting, Chloe was still relishing the fact that she had finally spoken out. And the best part was, nobody in town seemed the least bit mad at her. In fact, her rant actually made people like Chloe even more. The air felt considerably more friendly now that people knew she wasn't an emotionless robot.

As the cool autumn breezes threatened to blow in, Chloe began her annual fall cleaning spree with even more gusto than usual. Perched on a stepladder inside her backyard potting shed, Chloe scanned the floor for stray cats before reaching into the crawlspace and extracting a small cardboard box.

A feeling of familiarity flitted through her consciousness as she lifted the lid, exposing a chunk of butternut wood, expertly carved into the shape of a hovering, open-winged fairy. Chloe remembered watching Gramps as he sat on the back porch each evening, whittling scraps of wood into any shape she could imagine.

Flipping the fairy over, Chloe saw where Gramps had carved her own name along one wing. She knew exactly what she had to do, and fairly skipped down the path leading to the fairy garden.

The End

52967977R00114

Made in the USA
San Bernardino, CA
02 September 2017